"Am I such an ogre?" he asked.

Not waiting for an answer, Derek pulled her to him with a suddenness that made her gasp. His head came down, his lips seeking hers. She tried to turn away, but he cupped her chin with a hand that seemed to be made of steel.

Her struggles only served to wedge her more tightly between his arm and the unyielding strength of his chest, while he continued to kiss her as if he had all the time in the world. She became acutely aware of his firm, masculine body against her. Her lips softened as waves of unfamiliar feeling swept over her . . .

Dawnstar Romances

DAWNSTAR ROMANCE

Cinderella Charade

Angela Gadsden

GOLDEN APPLE PUBLISHERS

One

Samantha Fielding touched her tongue to lips gone dry and patted her cap of black curls nervously. She tugged at her blue linen skirt and wondered if she should have worn a dress instead of the severely tailored suit.

The receptionist, a woman in her sixties, smiled at Sam. "It shouldn't be much longer, Miss Fielding. Would you like a cup of coffee while you wait?"

"Oh, yes, thank you," Sam said. "I don't know why I'm so jittery . . ."

"Relax," the older woman said, handing her a styrofoam cup full of steaming black liquid. Her blue eyes seemed to twinkle with understanding. "You'll do just fine. I think you're exactly the type Mr. Spencer needs for this job."

Sam sipped the coffee gratefully and looked around the reception room. Judging from its appearance, Spencer Industries would be a pleasant place to work. The sofas and chairs were covered in cool tones of blue and green, and fresh plants added to the effect, making the room seem like a forest glade, a refuge from the steaming city streets outside.

Even in August, Sam loved Jacksonville. The heat of the Florida sun seemed to beckon her to silvery beaches and sparkling green water. Her tiny apartment was within walking distance of the ocean, and she liked nothing better than to walk along the shore adding to her shell collection, listening to the soothing murmur of the waves. Perhaps someday she would want to go back to Hollyville, the little town in Tennessee where she had grown up, but for now the memories were too fresh, too painful.

Sam stirred uneasily. Mrs. Hastings from the employment agency had been so vague about exactly what this job entailed. "Actually, Mr. Spencer was . . . well, it's a sort of public relations position. But, my dear, you must understand, Spencer Industries is a *most* reputable firm. You needn't worry about . . ." She had let her voice trail off, waving a hand as if shooing away all the dire fates Sam shouldn't worry about.

And now Sam *was* worried. Not about the terrible possibilities Mrs. Hastings's hemmings and hawings had conjured up, but about whether she was qualified for a public relations job. She had left college in her junior year to marry Kyle . . . don't think about that, she warned herself. Not yet, not now. You can't afford to get upset or rattled, Sam. You *need* this job.

Sam looked up as the door to Mr. Spencer's office opened. A tall, slender blonde walked out. Now that woman looked like a businesswoman, Sam thought. What chance did she have against someone like that?

The receptionist smiled and said, "You can go in now, Miss Fielding."

Sam approached the door timidly. Relax, girl, she

told herself sternly. Get it over with. Go in there, let him tell you the position has already been filled, and go look for something else. She took a deep breath and knocked on the door, then entered.

The office was large. Two walls were of smoked glass, offering a breathtaking view of Jacksonville and the St. Johns River. A massive desk stood beside one of the windows, and behind it a man sat, his chair swiveled around toward the view. Without turning, he called, "Have a seat, please. I'll be with you in a moment."

Sam perched on the seat of a leather armchair facing the desk, wondering if she was to be kept on pins and needles while her prospective employer sat gazing at the river. Then she heard the rustling of papers and realized he was reading—probably those recommendations she had imagined the other applicant providing.

The man turned and muttered, "Impossible," and tossed a folder onto the desk, scowling. Then he turned blue eyes on Sam, and she felt pinned like a butterfly by his gaze.

His hair was silver gray, crisply curling. His face was bronze, too young for hair so gray, too dark for eyes so blue, and Sam couldn't pull her own eyes away from him. He was the most handsome man she had ever seen.

"Miss Fielding?" he was saying, with the exaggerated patience of one who is repeating himself. "That *is* your name, isn't it?"

"What? Oh, yes, of course. Samantha Fielding. I . . . I've come about the job."

A silvery eyebrow arched in amusement. "I assumed as much, Miss Fielding. By the way, I'm Derek Spencer."

She nodded coolly, determined not to make a fool

3

of herself again. "I'm glad to meet you," she said quietly.

"Now that you've had a good look at me, Miss Fielding—"

Sam gasped. "Oh, Mr. Spencer, I'm so sorry—it's just . . . well, I've never seen anyone . . . your . . . that is, your eyes are so blue for one with your dark coloring. I didn't mean to stare. I mean it's very . . . attractive . . . I mean . . . ."

She was relieved when his laughter cut off her words, seeming to boom in the confines of the office. That laugh belonged on the open sea. Sam could imagine him at the wheel of a ship, laughing just like that in the face of a hurricane.

His laughter subsided, leaving only a twinkle in his eyes. "Haven't you ever looked in a mirror, Miss Fielding? Your own eyes are a very unusual shade of blue, hardly the color one expects to find under a mop of shiny black curls, you know. And I assure you, the combination is quite attractive on you, as well."

"Thank you. Mr. Spencer, I don't usually . . . blurt things out like this—"

"I understand. Job interviews make everyone nervous," he said gently. Then more crisply he added, "Now if you'd be so kind as to stand up, please."

Puzzled, she did as he asked. He rose and left his desk to circle her. Two spots of color appeared on her cheeks as she felt his scrutiny, wondering if he was paying her back for staring at him, but when he spoke his tone was businesslike. "Yes, I think you'll be fine."

She watched him as he returned to his desk. He was taller than she had realized, well over six feet. His chest and shoulders seemed too large to be confined to a suit, and again the image of him at sea came to her mind.

"Now, Miss Fielding, I'm sure there are some things you'd like to know about this . . . job. The most important fact is, it's temporary. Probably about six months. As I'm sure Mrs. Hastings told you, the pay is quite good. There will be some papers you must sign if you accept the position. By the way, do you like children?"

"What? Well, yes I do," Sam said, puzzled.

Derek Spencer reached for a framed photograph on his desk and turned it for Sam to see. "Good. This is my daughter Debby. She's nine years old, and you will see a good bit of her in the course of your . . . job. Things will be more pleasant for all of us if you two get along well."

Sam looked at the smiling young face of the little girl and returned the picture to Mr. Spencer. "She's very pretty. You must be proud of her," she said, and was dismayed to see a flash of pain cross his face.

"Yes," he said, dismissing the subject. "Well, the job is yours if you want it." He stood. "Do you have any questions?"

Sam rose from her chair, confused. "You mean just like that? Yes, of course I want it . . . I mean, oh, dear, I don't know exactly what the job is. Mrs. Hastings said it was something in public relations . . ."

Merriment filled his blue eyes. "I'm afraid I may have misled Mrs. Hastings a little. What the position is—Miss Fielding, I need a wife."

Sam felt the blood run from her face as she stared at him. "A . . . a wife?" she said, her voice hardly audible to her for the roaring in her ears. "Is this some kind of horrible joke? Did Kyle . . ." She felt her knees crumpling underneath her and stumbled to the sofa.

Derek Spencer leaned over her, a frown marring the tanned smoothness of his brow, and he spoke gently. "Just sit still, Miss Fielding. That was unforgivable of me—my clumsy idea of a joke."

"Did Kyle Bardwell put you up to this?" she asked icily.

The genuine bewilderment in his face at the mention of Kyle's name reassured her even before he spoke. "I don't know anyone by that name, Miss Fielding. The thing is—for legal reasons I won't go into, I need to be married. Just for a short time. I assure you, it wouldn't be a . . . a real marriage."

She slumped against the cushions, shaking her head. "Married," she said, smiling wryly. "You know, Mr. Spencer, I tried my best to convince myself I would be qualified for this position, but of all the jobs in the world you've come up with the one I'm least suited for. I'm sorry, I'm afraid I'm not very good at marriage!" she said firmly.

"Wait," he pleaded, seating himself beside her. "Listen to me. I don't know what problems you had in your marriage—I noticed on your application that you're divorced. But whatever the problems were, they won't have any bearing on this situation. This will be a business relationship."

The twinkle was gone from his eyes as he watched her seriously. Sam had a sudden realization that whatever this man's faults, lying was not one of them.

He went on. "Your duties will be to live in my house—you'll have your own room, of course—to go with me to social events as my wife, to act as a stepmother to my daughter. In short, to make it appear to the world at large that we are married. During this time you will draw a salary, and at the termination of the job you will receive a large lump sum payment."

Sam hesitated, hardly believing his words. She could never accept such a position—could she?

He glanced at his watch and rose, making a noise of impatience. "Damn—I almost forgot. I have an appointment. Look, it's right here in the building, so I should be back in twenty or thirty minutes. Why don't you wait here in my office? Just relax and think it over, all right?" Again his blue eyes caught hers with their amazing piercing quality, and she could only nod dumbly.

At the door he turned. "By the way, Miss Fielding, no one knows about this except the two of us and my receptionist, Mrs. Wright, who happens to be my aunt. It's absolutely imperative that I keep this confidential."

Sam nodded once more. "Yes, I understand." When the door closed behind him she sank back against the cushions of the sofa. Could she accept such a job? To marry a stranger?

A short, bitter laugh escaped her lips. Isn't that what you did last time, Sam? she asked herself. You certainly didn't know Kyle Bardwell as well as you thought you did.

And yet it seemed as if Kyle had always been in her life. He had come to Hollyville ten years ago, fresh out of college, and gone to work for her father in the Bank of Hollyville. Homer Fielding had taken an immediate liking to the ambitious young man, and he became a frequent visitor in the home Sam shared with her father.

Sam's mother had died when Sam was a baby. She had thought she and her father managed fairly well, just the two of them, but even at fifteen years old, Sam could see that in Kyle her father had found the son he never had. She came to think of Kyle as a big brother. He and her father together praised her fledgling efforts at gourmet cooking and chatted with her first suitors. The three of them went fishing together on weekends, and huddled around the television with bowls of popcorn during football season.

The change came when Sam went away to college. When she came home for weekends and vacations, she noticed that Kyle seemed to look at her with new eyes. The ease of brotherly affection was gone, replaced by a certain awkwardness. Homer Fielding noticed it immediately, and chuckled approvingly. He began going out to a penny ante poker game with some of his buddies several nights a week, and shooing Sam and Kyle out to a movie on other nights.

When Sam recognized her father's matchmaking for what it was, she was amused, but as time went by and Kyle began to press her, she began to wonder if he might not be the perfect husband for her. True, when he kissed her there was none of the dizzying excitement she had read about, but maybe such feelings only existed in books and movies. Wouldn't it be better to settle for a good man she had deep affection for, than to pursue a romantic fantasy? Sam had asked herself.

Kyle sensed her weakening, and pressed his advantage, driving up to college to visit her on the weekends she didn't come home, not giving her time to think. At the end of the fall term of her junior year, she packed her things up and came home to Hollyville. She and Kyle were married the week before Christmas.

The marriage was a disaster from the beginning. On their wedding night sunny, affectionate Kyle seemed to turn into a stranger. Sam watched his clear gray eyes darken with a passion her innocence had left her unprepared for, and Kyle was too impatient to give her time to accept this new side of him. His lovemaking was brief and brutal, leaving Sam shaking with restrained sobs, clinging to the edge of the mattress so as not to touch him.

In the next several weeks Sam tried to talk to her new husband about the problem, to persuade him to be gentle with her and give her time to match his passion, but to no avail. He became defensive, eager to place blame, and called her frigid.

They settled into a routine that was torture for Sam. When Kyle wanted her, she closed her eyes and gritted her teeth, longing to have it over with as quickly as possible. She learned to stifle any affectionate gestures she yearned to make toward him, because they inevitably led to the always humiliating, sometimes painful ritual of his lovemaking.

As miserable as Sam was, Kyle seemed content with their arrangement, enjoying the taunting jibes he made at her frigidity. Sam convinced herself that probably most marriages were like theirs. She had no one to confide in. Homer Fielding obviously believed Sam was as delighted with Kyle as he was, and she didn't have the heart to destroy his illusions. Besides, her face reddened at the very thought of talking to her father about sex. For the first time in years, Sam felt the loss of her mother keenly.

She cleaned their little house until it shone, and threw herself into community work as well. Somehow the months dragged by. She began to suspect that Kyle was seeing other women, a suspicion that became a certainty as he grew more and more careless. Looking back, Sam couldn't believe she had lived in this torment for three years. She wondered if she ever would have had the courage to leave if Kyle had restricted his betrayal to her. But he finally went too far—he betrayed the trust her father had put in him. ·

With Homer Fielding's encouragement and backing, Kyle had risen to a vice presidency in the Bank of Hollyville. The day he was arrested for embezzling bank funds, Sam saw her father turn into an old man. The members of the board of directors, the leaders of the community, all assured Homer Fielding that he was not to blame, but he couldn't forgive himself for letting his affection for Kyle blind him to the man's weakness.

Sam filed for divorce and stayed in Hollyville just long enough to see her father regain some of his old zest for life. Then she threw her suitcases into her little green Rabbit and left for Florida. She had meant to drive down the Atlantic coast to Miami, but fell in love with the crisp ocean breezes in Jacksonville.

In one frantically busy day she had found a studio apartment three blocks from the ocean, and a secretarial position with a beginning printing firm. For the past year her world had consisted of the office, her cozy home, and the ever-present, soothing roar of the Atlantic. When she was lonely she talked to her cat, Tiptoe, named for the fastidious way the animal picked its way across her dew-wet lawn, stopping frequently to lick each damp paw, only to set them down once again in moist grass.

It had been a calm, healing existence. But the printing firm, like so many new businesses, had gone into bankruptcy, and now Sam was out of a job.

So, she thought, sitting up straight on the leather couch, decision time. Could she really do this? Marriage! She shuddered involuntarily.

Not really a marriage, a calmer voice inside her asserted. A business deal, that's all. She'd been a good hostess, an immaculate housekeeper. She could cook. The only area of marriage where she had been a failure wouldn't be involved here.

But could she be sure? She agonized over it, remembering the blatant masculinity of Derek Spencer. His massive shoulders and chest making his business suit seem a silly trapping of civilization, totally out of place on his body—the panther-like stride Sam remembered uncomfortably—his undeniably striking good looks—

She stood abruptly. No, it was impossible. He must be used to having women throw themselves at his feet. A man like that . . . how could she live in the same house with him? How could she trust him not to expect. . . . She shuddered again.

And yet—those strangely blue eyes of his. When they twinkled with laughter, mischief peering from their depths, even she, who had thought herself immune to such feelings, felt his attraction. But when they were serious, it was impossible not to trust what she read in them. Concern, and honor. Yes, he was a man of honor. She was sure of that.

Rummaging in her handbag, Sam found her checkbook and looked at the balance she already had memorized: eighty-six dollars and forty-nine cents. Barely enough to get her back to Hollyville. Her apartment was paid for till the end of the week, and then she would have to come up with another month's rent.

Her apartment. If she took this position, she would have to give it up. But maybe she could sublet it, and with six months of no rent or utilities to pay, plus a salary—not to mention the lump sum payment when the job ended—she could build a nest egg large enough to last until she found a permanent job.

If only Derek Spencer were a mild-looking little man instead of so big, so disturbingly attractive. Torn by indecision, Sam wandered over to gaze through the smoked glass window at the river winding through the city. In the distance she could see palm trees waving lazily in the breeze along the highway that led, a few miles further along, to the ocean and her apartment. Her idiotic tabby cat was probably at this moment chasing his tail in circles around the living room. She smiled.

The office door opened and the receptionist walked in. "Derek told me you weren't feeling well, and I thought a hot cup of tea might help. Why don't you come over here and sit down with me for a few minutes?" She smiled warmly. Now that Sam knew she was Derek Spencer's aunt, she could see a family resemblance.

When Sam joined her on the sofa, she said, "My name is Trudy Wright. I'm Derek's aunt."

"Yes, I know," Sam said. "I was just noticing the resemblance."

"Oh, he told you that, did he? My word, the boy is getting positively talkative in his old age." She laughed. "Derek doesn't usually say anything that isn't absolutely necessary."

Sam smiled at the idea of anyone calling Derek Spencer a boy. Trudy Wright patted her hand gently. "Now, child, I hope you've decided to take this job. It's very important to Derek."

"Why is that, Mrs. Wright? Why does he need to pretend to be married?" Sam asked urgently.

The older woman shook her head. "No, dear. You'll have to ask Derek about that. He has a very good reason, but . . . anyhow, whether you take the job or not, call me Trudy. Even Aunt Trudy, if you feel you can manage it," she added, blue eyes twinkling exactly as her nephew's did.

"All right, Trudy, I—" Sam broke off as the door opened and a striking redhead entered the office. "Derek, are you—oh, Trudy. I thought Derek was in here." She stood in the doorway, her brows raised in questioning arches.

Sam had never seen such a beautiful woman. From the top of her flaming red hair to the toes of her alligator pumps, she was flawless. Her expensively cut suit was the same shade of green as her eyes, eyes that narrowed slightly as she looked at Sam.

"Have you ever thought of knocking, G.G.? No, Derek's not here," Trudy said dryly. "You're his secretary, you should know he has an appointment with Paul Grinder today. He's upstairs now. That's Derek's dentist," Trudy explained to Sam.

A giggle rose to Sam's lips. "A dentist named Grinder?"

Trudy's eyes shone with laughter. "I know. Don't you just love it? We tease Paul about it all the time."

The redheaded woman walked across to the sofa— no, she doesn't walk, Sam thought. She glides. She extended a hand with long scarlet nails and said, "I don't believe we've met. And don't listen to that silly G.G. business of Trudy's—my name is Gloria, Gloria Lanahan."

Touching her cool hand briefly, Sam said, "I'm Samantha Fielding. I'm—"

"She's a good friend of Derek's," Trudy interjected. "From Atlanta."

Again those green eyes narrowed. "A good friend of Derek's? How strange—I've never heard him mention your name."

"Well, I . . . I haven't known him very long," Sam said.

"That must be why then," Gloria said. "I thought I knew all his friends."

"Oh, you'll have plenty of chances to get to know Samantha," Trudy said sweetly. "She's going to be around here quite a bit, aren't you, dear?" she asked, swiveling toward Sam.

Turning from twinkling blue eyes to probing green ones, Sam voiced the decision she knew she had already made. "Oh, yes. I expect to be around here quite a bit."

"Wonderful!" Trudy exclaimed. "Now, G.G., if you'll excuse us, Samantha and I have a lot to talk about, and I'm sure you have things to do."

Gloria left with ill-concealed irritation, slamming the door slightly behind her. Trudy's face showed delight as she poured another cup of tea for herself and Sam. It was obvious she and her nephew's secretary were not the best of friends.

"Why do you call her G.G.?" Sam asked.

Trudy chuckled. "Because it irritates her, and because it fits. It stands for Gorgeous Gloria."

Sam shook her head. "She's gorgeous all right."

Trudy snorted. "She ought to be! Every waking minute of that girl's life is spent in glamorizing herself. Outside, beautiful—inside, empty. Nothing there. Ahh!" she said in disgust. "Her rich father buys her those expensive clothes so that she can take a job she doesn't need, and for one reason only—to catch a richer husband!"

Sam sipped the tea, watching Trudy. The older woman seemed to replay her own words in her mind. Her voice softened. "Maybe I'm not being entirely fair. It's just that she's after Derek, and I'm a little protective of my nephew. He's already had one wife like that, he doesn't need another!"

Sam looked into her cup and sighed. "She's not going to like me very well, then. She doesn't know. . ."

"No, and she can't know! You and I and Derek are the only ones who are to know that this marriage is a business arrangement!" Trudy tapped Sam's hand for emphasis, then lowered her voice. "Child, I can tell you're not used to deceit, and it goes against the grain for me, too. But it's important—you're going to be doing something wonderful for Derek, Samantha."

Sam looked at the woman's kind face and felt the same certainty as before, with Derek Spencer, that here was a person of honor. "Trudy, please call me Sam. No one calls me Samantha."

Trudy hooted. "Sam! Now that's some name for a pretty, frilly little thing like you. I love it! Sam!"

They sat for some time talking about the oddities of names, how some fit and some didn't, which led to Sam's telling Trudy how she had chosen Tiptoe's name, and they discovered they shared a love of cats. It had been months since Sam had a friend to talk to, and she found herself hoping she and Trudy would be friends long after this strange new job came to an end.

They were laughing over Sam's story of Tiptoe's encounter with a neighbor's lawn sprinkler when Derek Spencer returned, his bulk seeming to fill the doorway of the office. "Well," he said, "from the sound of things in here, I'd say you have good news for me. Right, Aunt Trudy?"

Two

Trudy rose from the sofa and gathered the tea cups, "Now, Derek, don't be so impatient. My word, you're always in such a hurry! I'll just leave you two to talk about that." Though her words were scolding, there was no mistaking the fondness in her tone. At the door she looked back and made a tsk-tsk sound at her nephew. "Always in a hurry, my, my."

Derek Spencer smiled, shaking his head, and moved to his desk. Sam sat down across from him, grinning in appreciation of Trudy.

He leaned back in his chair, tapping his fingers nervously against its padded arms. He *is* impatient, Sam thought. "Well, Miss Fielding, what have you decided?"

Sam drew a deep breath. "I've decided to take the job."

Derek Spencer slapped the palms of his hands on the gleaming surface of his desk. "Great! Now, there are some details to be ironed out."

"Wait—" Sam said, suddenly feeling rushed by his

brisk efficiency. A most impatient man, she thought, her misgivings rising.

At her protest he sat back in watchful repose. Sam detected a glint of amusement in his blue eyes as a silver brow arched quizzically. "I . . . I still have a few questions," she said.

He nodded, his gaze never releasing her own. "Yes?"

"To begin with, why are you doing this?"

A curtain seemed to drop across his face, closing her out. "That needn't concern you, Miss Fielding. Either you accept the job or you don't. My reasons are my own." His tone admitted no room for argument.

Resigned, Sam nodded. "All right. But why me? Is there some reason you chose me for this . . . position?"

Now the amusement was back in his gaze. "Because you're the most gorgeous creature I've ever seen, and I want to get you in my power and take you off somewhere and ravish you."

At her gasp his face became grave. "My God, is that really what you're afraid of?" He leaned over the desk to peer at her closely. "Miss Fielding, I can't tell you my reasons for this . . . this charade, but I do have them. As for why I chose you—there were several points that influenced that decision."

He leaned back once more, tapping a folder Sam knew contained her application for this bizarre job. "The ages are right, believable. You're twenty-five years old, I'm thirty-four—a good difference for a marriage, I think. Remember, I want people to believe that we really are married, that we're in love."

She nodded. "Yes, I understand that."

"Good. Furthermore, you have no relatives or close friends in Florida who might ask awkward questions about such a sudden marriage. I've cooked up a story to tell my friends and business associates about our whirlwind courtship, by the way. Trudy is my only living relative, and I've never had a secret yet I wouldn't trust her with."

Sam nodded again. Derek Spencer leaned back in his chair and rubbed his eyes. looking suddenly weary. "There are other reasons as well. You really *are* beautiful, and to be honest, people who know me well would expect me to marry a beautiful woman. I'm known as a great admirer of beauty," he said, grinning at her.

To her surprise, Sam grinned back, for some reason not feeling at all threatened by his open admiration. Then he sighed. "But there are lots of beautiful women. The thing about you is you're such a little bit of a thing—how tall *are* you?"

"Five-two," Sam said.

"And every bit of a hundred pounds, right?"

"Ninety-eight. But I don't see what that—"

"I've been married once. It was pretty bad. Vicky was tall, statuesque. She was beautiful, but only on the outside."

Sam started as he echoed Trudy's words. "You're divorced, then?"

He shook his head. "No, she was killed in a car accident. We were separated at the time, had been for months. My father had taken her to dinner, trying to work out a reconciliation."

He rubbed his eyes again. "Dammit, I had told him I didn't want her back. If only—she was driving, and evidently she had had too much to drink. She went into a railroad crossing, with all the lights flashing—" He stopped, as if to gain control of his voice. "I don't know, maybe she did it on purpose. She was self-destructive, and if she could hurt me at the same time by taking Dad with her—so much the better." He slammed a fist against his desk.

Sam felt her eyes filling with tears. "Mr. Spencer, I'm sorry. I shouldn't have asked—"

He gave her a half-smile. "You couldn't have known. Anyhow, I guess I wanted to pick someone as unlike Vicky as possible. I know that really doesn't make much sense, but affairs of the heart usually don't, and, remember, that's what this must seem to be."

"Of course," Sam said quietly, moved by his pain. She tried to think of something to say to divert him from unhappy memories, but absurdly found herself wanting only to pat the hand that lay, still clenched into a fist, on his desk.

"I'm sure you'll have things you need to take care of. You'll have most of the week," he went on in a businesslike tone.

"Oh—Tiptoe! Mr. Spencer, I have a cat. I really don't want to give him up. Do you think—I mean, he's housebroken and neutered. He does have claws, though, and I know what that does to furniture—"

She broke off as she saw his wide grin. "A cat— you really are different from Vicky. She couldn't stand animals. Bring him with you. I know Debby will love it."

Sam breathed a sigh of relief.

"Now," he went on. "We need to get our stories straight on this courtship. By the way, no one's going to believe we're just two happy kids in love if you keep calling me Mr. Spencer," he said dryly. "The name is Derek."

"All right, Derek. I'm Sam."

For a moment there was silence as he stared at her blankly. Then the booming laughter she remembered from their first interview once again filled the office. "Sam! Sam!"

She sat smiling tolerantly, waiting for him to finish guffawing. Really, she thought, this man does not belong in a city. Before she could enjoy her moment of feeling smugly superior, however, he sobered and looked at her intently, his eyes still holding traces of tears from his laughter. He reached across the desk to grasp her hands.

"Now hear this, young lady. There is no way, absolutely *no* way I am going to marry someone named Sam. You are Samantha, understood?"

Bridling, Sam said, "Now *you* hear this, Mr. Spenc—Derek. My father has always called me Sam, my friends call me Sam, and that's what I call myself. I'll change my last name, but not my first!"

For a long moment he stared at her, then pushed his chair back abruptly and went to gaze out at the river, hands thrust into his pockets. Finally he turned and came back to perch on the edge of his desk, facing Sam. He leaned over and grasped her chin in two strong fingers, forcing her to look up at him. She could see anger and humor struggling together in his eyes. "All right. Your father may call you Sam, and all your friends may, but *I'll* call you Samantha. Stubborn Samantha!"

"That's big of you, letting my father and my friends call me Sam," she said dryly. "Thank you."

Now humor won the battle going on in Derek's face, and he chuckled, still holding her chin. His eyes dropped for the briefest of moments to her lips, and Sam stiffened, sure he was about to kiss her. He seemed to sense her reaction, and released her. "You're welcome," he said smoothly, deliberately not recognizing her sarcasm. "I like to be tolerant about unimportant things."

Sam stifled a gasp of anger when she saw him watching her closely, and realized he was baiting her. He went back to sit behind his desk, shaking his head and grinning. "Sam Spencer—my God! The last person I knew who was named Sam was a three-hundred-pound foreman who used to work for me."

"Well, now you have a one-hundred-pound employee named Sam," she said coolly.

"Ninety-eight pounds, wasn't it? Your fighting weight, I presume, slugger?" He shook his head again. "And you look like such a sweet, timid little thing. Ah, well. Back to business, *Samantha.* Today is Monday. We'll be married in Atlanta on Friday, then fly to Puerto Rico for a few days. I have to go to Atlanta frequently on business, so we'll tell people we met there a few weeks ago, and it was love at first sight. All right?"

"All right. Oh!" Sam suddenly remembered Gloria Lanahan's questions. "But doesn't your secretary go with you on these trips?" she asked.

Barely concealed laughter was in Derek's voice as he looked at her with interest. "Are you inquiring into the nature of my relationship with my secretary, Samantha? Really, we aren't even married yet!"

"Of course not," she answered, flushing. "It's just that I met her a few minutes ago, and she mentioned that she knew all your friends—"

"You met Gloria? Damn," he muttered. "I deliberately arranged errands for her to keep her out of the building until this was settled. This complicates things."

"It may not. Your Aunt Trudy told her I was a good friend of yours from Atlanta. And I said I had only known you a short time, so that should fit in with your story."

He smiled, relief in his tone. "Wonderful. You and Aunt Trudy saved the day."

"Trudy told Gloria that I would be around here quite a bit, so . . ."

"Better and better," he said, beaming. "What could

be more natural than the woman I'm going to marry visiting the Jacksonville office? Yes, it makes sense. You two handled that situation beautifully."

Sam found his approval ridiculously intoxicating. What a mercurial man he was, she thought. Storm clouds of anger one moment, rays of sunshine the next. Abruptly she found herself wondering why he didn't want his secretary to know the truth. What *was* the nature of their relationship?

She looked up to find his penetrating gaze on her. "Any more questions?" he drawled, and she wondered if he had read her mind.

"No," she said hastily.

"All right. As I said, we'll be married in Atlanta on Friday, but I think we should fly into town on Wednesday evening so that you can spend Thursday shopping. You're a lovely woman, but your taste in clothes—what is a pretty, feminine woman like you doing in such a drab suit? You belong in something soft, wafting along on a cloud of perfume."

Sam stared at him, speechless. Her closet at home was full of the kind of clothes he described, her favorite styles. The man was infuriatingly perceptive.

"Look, Derek, I happen to like ruffles just fine, but not for a job interview. After all, when I came in here this morning I thought this was a legitimate, businesslike firm, not a . . . a mail-order bride business!"

His chuckle told her he had won a point for her anger. "Easy, Samantha. Or maybe you're right, maybe Sam does fit you better."

"Why do you do that?" she asked in exasperation. "Do you like to make people angry?"

"Not everyone," he answered easily. "I suppose it would just make you madder if I said it's because you're so pretty when you're angry."

Sam glared at him stonily.

"All right, Samantha. It's just that you remind me of a kitten who thinks she's a tiger. You bare your claws and don't realize how—" He stopped. "Let's just say I like your style, okay?"

Slightly mollified, but not quite trusting him, Sam said, "Okay."

"As far as your wardrobe is concerned, I'm sure it's fine. But I want to be seen with you in Atlanta. I want the society pages to carry photographs of Derek Spencer and his bride-to-be shopping for a trousseau. Everything I can do to lend credence to our story, I want to do."

Sam's face softened as she realized the validity of what he was saying. "This is terribly important to you, isn't it?"

He nodded somberly. "Yes. The most important thing in the world."

"Then of course I'll do whatever you say."

"Good," he said, eyes twinkling. "I'm glad you're not going to fight me on *every* point." Before she could reply he pushed the button on his intercom and said, "Aunt Trudy, would you tell Ned that Samantha and I are ready for those papers now? The two of you can sign as witnesses."

Then he leaned back in his swivel chair. "Ned Palmer, that's my attorney, Samantha, is right upstairs, so we'll have the contract in just a moment."

"Your lawyer's in this building, too?"

He grinned. "I hate driving in the city. The open road is one thing, but all that stop and go, stop and go, of city driving—I try to avoid it." Once again Sam noticed his long brown fingers tapping on his chair, and could imagine his impatience with traffic lights and crowded city streets. She shook her head. Clearly, Derek Spencer was not a patient man. He seemed to be a tightly wound bundle of pent-up energy.

There was a light tap on the door and Trudy entered, followed by a slightly built middle-aged man whom Derek introduced as Ned Palmer. Mr. Palmer went over the papers with Sam, answering her questions. It seemed that all the contract did was assure that she would give Derek a divorce in six months, and that she would be given a generous lump sum settlement. The only further stipulation was that she tell no one of their agreement. She and Derek signed the original and copies for each of them, with Mr. Palmer and Trudy signing as witnesses.

As Trudy and Mr. Palmer left the office, Sam could see Gloria at her desk in the reception room, her green eyes alight with curiosity. When the door closed, Derek said, "Well, that about does it. Can you close up your apartment and be ready by Wednesday evening?"

Sam hesitated. "I don't see why not. My landlady will take care of Tiptoe for a few days, I think. She adores him. And there's not that much to pack. It's a furnished apartment."

"Good. I'll send someone by there Wednesday to bring your things to my home, and I'll pick you up at six o'clock Wednesday night. Our flight leaves at seven. And that's it," he said, nodding briskly.

Sam stood. "Then I guess I'd better be going. I have a lot to do."

He rose and came around the desk. "Not so fast. Remember, we're in love." Before Sam understood his words, he had a huge arm wrapped around her shoulders as he opened the door to the outer office. In full view of Gloria and Trudy, he planted a kiss on her lips, his arm tightening vise-like when she tried to pull away. "I'll see you soon, darling," he said, loud enough for the women to hear, his eyes warning Sam.

Belatedly aware of Gloria's scrutiny, Sam smiled up at him. "Soon, dear," she said sweetly. His chuckle was too low to reach any ears but hers.

Three

The next two days went by in a haze for Sam. Mrs. Hotchkiss, her landlady, was delighted to keep Tiptoe for her. Sam found packing her belongings went more quickly than she had expected. She was surprised at how little she had accumulated in the last year, but then she had never been acquisitive. That had been another area of disagreement between her and Kyle. Her husband had been impatiently eager to obtain what he called the finer things of life. For Sam, there was nothing finer in the world than the ocean that whispered to her constantly in her tiny apartment.

Wednesday afternoon she looked around the place, now strangely empty-looking. Her things had been sent to Derek's home, except for one small suitcase she had packed for the trip to Atlanta and Puerto Rico. My wedding trip, she thought shakily, and then firmly turned her mind to other things.

She picked up Tiptoe. In the manner of cats, he let himself hang limply over her arm, purring. "Well, friend," she said, rubbing his orange fur against her cheek, "it's time to take you to Mrs. Hotchkiss, but I'll be back in a few days. And you'll have a new home to investigate. You know how you love exploring." Yellow eyes blinked at her sleepily. "A new adventure for both of us, Tiptoe, and it's time to get started, before I lose my nerve."

With a firm step, Sam walked down the hall to Mrs. Hotchkiss's apartment. The landlady made a great fuss over Tiptoe, which he tolerated gracefully for a few moments. When he had all the attention he could stand, he sauntered out the open door to the patio and climbed onto a sunny redwood table to nap.

"He'll be just fine here, Miss Fielding. Oh, and I have some wonderful news for you! I've already rented your apartment, which means you'll get some of your rent money back, of course. But best of all, the gentleman who rented it only wants it for six months!"

"What? Oh, Mrs. Hotchkiss, that's almost too good to be true! Then I'll be able to get it back?"

"You certainly will, dear. You and Tiptoe have been model tenants, I must say."

"Oh, I'm so relieved," Sam said. "When is the new tenant moving in?"

A frown creased Mrs. Hotchkiss's soft white forehead. "Well, that bothers me just a little. He said he wouldn't be moving in, that he just wanted an apartment near the beach to use from time to time. For business reasons, he said. You don't think he wants it as a . . . a love nest, do you?"

Sam smothered a smile at the landlady's use of the old-fashioned term. "Probably not, Mrs. Hotchkiss. Perhaps he has business associates coming in from out of town who want to stay at the beach while they're here."

Mrs. Hotchkiss seemed relieved. "Yes, that's probably it. I must admit, Mr. Palmer didn't seem the type to—"

Sam's eyes narrowed. "Mr. Palmer? That wouldn't be Ned Palmer, would it?"

"Why, yes. Why, dear? Do you know him?" Mrs. Hotchkiss asked, surprised.

"Not really. I just recognize the name. He's an attorney for—he's an attorney," she said, flustered.

After a final peek at her cat, Sam went back to her apartment. Ned Palmer had rented it for six months! Surely this was no coincidence—he must have been acting on Derek's instructions. And yet Derek hadn't said a word to her about it. Touched by his thoughtfulness, Sam began to dress for the trip.

Remembering Derek's taunt about her severely tailored suit, she had chosen a dress of soft peach silk for the flight to Atlanta. The vee neckline had a wide ruffle that framed her face gently. Her hair, still damp from her shower, curled in shining tendrils at her temples. A touch of mascara to emphasize wide blue eyes, a light coat of lip gloss to match her dress, and Sam was pleased with her appearance. She noted with approval that the fullness of her skirt seemed to add a much-needed few pounds to her slender frame, while at the same time adding a glow to her new tan. A final touch of perfume—to waft along in, she thought wryly, remembering Derek's words again—and she was ready.

When the doorbell rang, she picked up her suitcase and her handbag as she went to answer it. She didn't want to keep an impatient man like Derek Spencer waiting, or have him accuse her of not being ready on time.

His eyes widened as she opened the door. "Well!" he breathed. "Oh, yes, you will do very nicely for this job."

She smiled in acknowledgement of his compliment, and walked with him to the silver-gray Mercedes he had parked at the curb. In spite of his comments about city driving, he drove expertly. Sam relaxed against the plush seat and watched his profile, the shadows of twilight playing on his strong features. There was a great deal more to this man than met the eye, she thought, and remembered her conversation with Mrs. Hotchkiss.

"Derek, did you have Ned Palmer rent my apartment?" she asked, watching his face in the shifting light.

"Now how did you find out about that?" he asked, turning to glance at her. "I didn't mean for you to know until your job was over."

"That was very nice of you."

He concentrated on the increasing traffic as he spoke, not looking at her. "Well, you spoke of it so fondly—I hated for you to lose it on my account," he said, rather gruffly. Then, as if to change the subject, "Damn these red lights. I hope we don't miss our plane."

Sam smiled and said softly, "Thank you, Derek."

"Don't give it another thought. How's your cat—all safely tucked away with your landlady?"

"Yes," Sam said, and began telling Derek about Tiptoe's antics. It turned out that Derek, during his boyhood, had enjoyed a succession of pets that included several cats, a beagle, and a skunk. Their conversation for the remainder of the drive was liberally sprinkled with laughter.

It wasn't until they were safely aboard the jet, fastening their seat belts, that Sam looked at the man beside her and thought that when they made the flight back they'd be married! This . . . stranger would be her husband!

Calm down, Sam, her inner voice scolded. He won't really be your husband; he'll be a . . . a business partner, an employer, that's all.

Derek misinterpreted the sudden tension on her face, and covered her hand with his. "Takeoffs make you nervous, Samantha?" he asked gently.

She looked at him intently, but could find no trace of laughter in his clear blue eyes. "Uh . . . yes, I guess they do." She forced herself to leave her hand clasped in his, trying to ignore the warm strength of his lean, brown fingers.

The flight was smooth, and it seemed a very short time later to Sam that she found herself in a luxurious hotel room high above the city lights of Atlanta. She was suddenly exhausted, and nervous to know that Derek had the adjoining room. Very quietly, so that he wouldn't hear, she checked the connecting door to make sure it was locked.

You foolish ninny, she chided herself silently. You're going to be living in this man's house—you'd better trust him or back out before it's too late!

She jumped as a light tap sounded on the door between her room and Derek's. "Yes?" she called.

His voice seemed full of rather exaggerated patience. "Would you open the door please, Samantha? I'd like to speak to you."

She opened the door and stood fingering the collar of her dress nervously. He had changed to a loose fitting creamy silk shirt and casual brown slacks. "I wondered if you would want to share a late supper with me," he said. "I'm tired, and would rather have room service send something up than to go out. Would that suit you?"

For the first time, Sam realized that she was hungry. "Yes, I'd like that, thank you," she said.

"Good. You have time, if you'd like to change into something—" He stopped, and leered at her. "—something more comfortable."

Outraged, she had her hand on the door, ready to slam it in his face, when he laughed and caught it. "Oh, Samantha, don't you know I'm kidding you? Look, if it will make you feel . . . safer, I'll call you Sam "

His laughter was irresistible, and suddenly Sam felt she was foolish to be afraid of him. She began to laugh too. "Now that's better," he said. "And I really did think you might want to put on something more casual. If you're anything like me, when you're tired you don't feel like being dressed up. Gorgeous as you look in that dress, I thought you might prefer slacks or jeans or something. But that's up to you, I just want you to know I'm not really the big, bad wolf, okay?"

"Okay, Derek," she said. "I'll be with you in a few minutes."

She had a pair of blue silk lounging pajamas she had bought early in her marriage to Kyle. She wasn't sure why she had packed them for this trip, unless it was that Derek's remarks about her clothes had made her pack her most feminine things. Now she examined them critically. They weren't the least bit sexy, she decided. Not at all improper for her to wear to a late supper in his room.

She put them on and looked in the mirror. The neck was high, with a mandarin collar, the sleeves were long, and they were not form-fitting—but the color exactly matched her eyes and they rustled when she moved, and she loved wearing them. She ran a comb through her cap of curls and knocked on Derek's door.

"Come in," he said, standing aside to let her enter. "Wow," he added softly. "I suppose that's what you wear for gardening, and painting cupboards, you know—all those little chores around the house?"

"They're comfortable," she said, shrugging.

"Oh. And I'm sure you didn't know they turn your eyes the most amazing shade of cornflower blue?" he said, grinning. "I hope you don't mind, I've ordered for both of us. It should be here any minute."

He led her to a huge white sofa in the center of the room, and they sat down. "Listen, Samantha—Sam," he said, bowing toward her, "now when the food comes I need to put my arm around you, act affectionate. Don't forget, we're playing a part, both of us."

His eyes on her were serious. "Yes, you're right, of course," she said. "I'll remember."

Even so, when the waiters rolled in a table and Derek seated her, caressing her shoulder as he did so, it took all her control not to pull away from his hand. My God, she thought, is this what Kyle did to me? She could tell Derek felt her resistance, and his mouth tightened with annoyance.

When they were alone, however, the tension in the air lessened. They ate their cold supper of chicken and wine and fruit, talking companionably, and Sam was surprised to find she was enjoying herself. She found that Derek shared one of her deepest feelings, her almost mystic love of the ocean.

"After Dad died, and Vicky, I thought I'd go crazy for a while," he said. "I blamed myself for Dad's death, you see. But I would walk along the shore and listen to that constant rumble of the waves . . ." He shook his head, remembering.

"I know just what you mean," Sam said. "There's a sort of . . . healing quality about it."

He turned to her. "Yes, that's it exactly. Now whenever I'm troubled, I go out and listen to what the ocean has to say about it."

Sam smiled. "I've never heard it put like that, but, yes . . . I can understand."

He poured them another glass of wine. When he handed it to her, his hand brushed hers, and Sam drew back immediately. She hoped he hadn't noticed her involuntary movement.

For a moment he was silent, then he said quietly, "Are you afraid of men, Samantha? Or is it just me?"

"Oh, Derek," she said miserably. "I'm sorry, I know it's ridiculous . . ."

"Is it because of something that happened in your marriage?"

"Yes," Sam whispered. "I suppose it is."

"Do you want to talk about it?" He moved as if to touch her hand, then stopped himself.

She looked up at him, blue eyes filling with tears. "No, Derek. I don't think I could talk to . . . to anyone about it."

"All right. But remember, we're going to be spending a lot of time together, and I'm a good listener. I don't hurt birds with broken wings, Samantha. Or step on kittens, even if they do bare their claws." He smiled and his eyes were gentle.

Sam felt the tears threatening to spill over, and knew that the combination of tension and exhaustion had her on the edge of sobs. "I think I'd better go, Derek," she said shakily. "I'm very tired."

"Yes," he agreed, opening the door for her. In her room, without thinking, she snapped the lock between them. Then she put her hand to her mouth in embarrassment, hoping he hadn't heard, wondering if he was laughing at her "maidenly" fears.

There was no sign of unhappy emotions in Derek at breakfast the next morning. He was enthusiastic, full of plans for the day. "Now, Samantha," he said, "it's only natural that your bridegroom-to-be would want to spoil you, so enjoy it. I'm going to play the part to the hilt, buying you beautiful clothes. I'm going to be such a doting fiancé I'll be disgusting." He grinned at her happily.

She couldn't resist grinning back. "Do you always do things so wholeheartedly?"

"Absolutely. Now finish your breakfast. There's a very good dress shop I want to start with. My mother and Trudy bought most of their things there when we used to live in Atlanta."

"Did your—never mind," Sam amended hastily.

"Did my wife shop there?" Derek's lip curled. "Only once or twice. Colette is too good at seeing through people like Vicky, and it made her uncomfortable. Colette is a little Frenchwoman about a hundred years old, and she can spot a phony in a second."

"Aren't you afraid she'll realize we aren't really . . . well, in love?"

"On that point, I have every intention of fooling those sharp old eyes, Samantha."

Colette's place was located on a side street in a very exclusive section of Atlanta. It was one of those shops Samantha would never have ventured into, knowing at a glance the prices would be completely outside her budget. They were just inside the door when a tiny bird of a woman came chirping toward them. "Derek! But how wonderful! It has been so long. Come, come! Sit down and I will have Marietta bring us some tea. I was so sorry to hear about your mother—what, two years ago now, wasn't it? And Trudy—how is my old friend? And who is this lovely lady—a girl friend, no? She is far too pretty to be a wife!"

Derek's laughter boomed in the tiny shop, and Colette pressed her hands together, beaming at him. "That laugh of yours, Derek! It is the thing I always remember the most about you. How refreshing it is after the ladylike teehees I hear all day. The laughter of a man, no, chickadee?" she said, touching Sam's arm. "Ah, thank you, Marietta," she added, as a smiling teenager brought out a tea tray.

Over cups of the fragrant brew, Colette said, "Now, Derek, what can I do for you? Did you bring this enchanting woman here for a wardrobe? I heard you had separated from your first wife, and I must admit I was glad. She was not good enough for you, I always knew it. Ah, but this one," she said, beaming at Sam. "You are getting married, no? I can always tell when people are in love. There is a certain feeling in the air, an . . . electricity. I am right, no?"

Derek arched an eyebrow at Sam, grinning. "You're right, Colette. And I've already told Samantha I intend to spoil her, so we'll want to see your most beautiful things—dresses, gowns, and sportswear."

"And, of course, lingerie—for the honeymoon," Colette added, her brown eyes sparkling wickedly. Sam's blush delighted her. Sam could gladly have kicked Derek, for she could see from the mischief in his eyes how much he was enjoying this.

The next hours passed by in a giddy whirl for Sam. Colette brought out dress after dress for her to try on, each one lovelier than the last. For the most part, they fit perfectly. In the few cases where alterations were needed, Colette did them herself in a matter of minutes, her tiny fingers flying along the beautiful fabrics. There were cocktail dresses and casual dresses and very formal gowns. There were slacks, shorts and bathing suits, blouses and halter tops. Derek's vocabulary seemed to consist of three words: "We'll take it."

Once when Colette was out of the room, Sam tried to protest at his extravagance, but he laid a finger on her lips and shook his head warningly. Just then Colette came hurrying back, and to Sam's dismay, she carried a filmy peignoir and nightgown set.

"As soon as I saw you, I thought of this," she said to Sam, holding the lacy gown out to her. "It is the same shade as your eyes."

"You would need a very deep shade of pink to match her cheeks right now, Colette," Derek chuckled. "I need to make some calls; if I could excuse myself to use your telephone, it might be less awkward for my fiancée to select the lingerie she would like."

"But of course, Derek. You know where my office is. Please make yourself at home."

Sam pushed the gown aside. "Really, Derek, I couldn't—"

In a second he was beside her, hands on her shoulders, his icy blue gaze stopping her words. "Now, darling," he said teasingly, "if you won't select them, I'll do it for you. Do you have anything black and lacy, Colette?" he asked, chuckling, but his eyes never released Sam's.

"I . . . I think I'd rather choose them myself, Derek," Sam said, gently enough, but her blue eyes shot angry darts back at him.

A corner of his mouth turned down in amusement, but he made his voice sincere—for Colette's benefit—

when he said, "And now, darling, as much as I hate leaving you even for a second, I'd better make those phone calls." He planted a soft kiss on Sam's lips, while Colette smiled approvingly, then turned and left for Colette's office.

"Ah! Such a romantic man—but I don't have to tell you, do I?" Colette sighed. "The way you look at him, it is obvious . . ."

Sam turned to her, stunned, still feeling the heat of Derek's lips on her own. "What? Oh, yes, he's quite a romantic man." What did Colette see in the way she looked at Derek? If she felt anything for the man, it was that she'd like to throttle him for putting her in this spot and enjoying it so thoroughly!

"Now this gown really would be perfect for you," Colette went on. "And the peignoir—see how soft and feminine it is? You will be a vision in it!"

It was lovely, Sam thought, touching the delicate lace. And if she tried to buy her usual single girl nightshifts and pajamas, Colette would wonder. Aloud she said, "Yes, I think I'd like this one, Colette."

"Good. And I have another you might like," she said, and disappeared into the other room.

When Colette returned with the next gown, Sam's eyes widened. If Derek wanted something black and lacy, this would certainly fill the bill, she thought. But what was she thinking? Derek would never see these! A tiny pang of something that could have been regret registered on the corner of her mind for a fleeting instant, then she pushed it aside.

"Wow!" she said, touching the diaphanous material. "It's quite . . . revealing, isn't it?"

"It is flagrantly sexy," Colette said cheerfully. "Sounds like the name of a perfume, no? But why not? You have the figure for it."

Joking to cover her embarrassment, Sam said, "It looks so delicate. It probably wouldn't wear very well."

Devilment filled Colette's shoe-button eyes. "It will wear for years, chérie. Believe me, you will never have it on for more than a few minutes at a time—then whoosh," she said, making a motion of drawing a garment over her head, "it's off!"

Her cackle of laughter was so open and friendly that Sam couldn't resist joining in. Colette patted Sam's shoulder and her voice softened. "Derek is a very . . . manly man. He will love this. And you, little one, should not be afraid or ashamed with him. Can you not see how tender he is with you? You are a beautiful bird, and you must fly!"

Tears sprang to Sam's eyes at the kindness in the older woman's tone. She felt guilty at deceiving her, and strangely wistful. How wonderful it would be if she and Derek were what they pretended to be—Cinderella and her Prince Charming. If she had had someone like this wise old lady to talk to when she really *was* a bride, perhaps things might have been different . . .

"Now, what are these long faces about?" Derek said, coming through the door. "Have you two been having a serious talk? None of that now. This is a day for celebrating," he said jubilantly, sweeping Sam into his arms and spinning with her about the room. "I hope there are some beautiful gowns for dancing in your collection, because I intend to take my fiancée out on the town tonight, Colette!"

"You're right, Derek," Colette said as he set Sam on her feet, slightly out of breath. "This is a time for celebrating, and there are several lovely gowns to choose from."

"Choose? Choose? Of course not—we'll take them all!" he said, laughing.

"Now, Derek, really. That's ridiculous," Sam said, with some heat. "I'll select the one I like best, and that's enough."

He looked at her with surprise, then a smile spread across his face. "Do you hear that?" he asked, turning to Colette. "She's turning into a wife right before my eyes!"

"Someone needs to save you from yourself, Derek. Be grateful," Colette said, shaking a bony finger at him.

Sam only took a few moments to select one final gown, suddenly aghast at the amount of money Derek was spending. When they were about to leave Colette's shop, he walked back and said a few quiet words to her, embracing her warmly.

The tall buildings were casting long shadows across the sidewalks when they emerged from the shop, and Sam was surprised to realize that it was late afternoon. "That went well, don't you think?" Derek asked as they walked down the block looking for a taxi. They carried only a few dress boxes; Colette had promised to have the rest at the hotel the next morning.

"She believed us, if that's what you mean. But Derek, you shouldn't have bought so many things. It wasn't necessary."

"I suppose not. But to be honest, Samantha, I guess I feel a little guilty about you."

She turned to look at him as they walked, surprised. "Guilty! Why?"

He shrugged. "Oh, I don't know. It just seems a little highhanded to hire someone, knowing it's only for six months, and expect them to turn their whole world topsy-turvy for you. Giving up your apartment—"

"Which you promptly rented, so I could have it back," she reminded him dryly.

"Yes, but I know this pretence is hard on you, and I like to think the new wardrobe, as well as lending credence to our story, is a sort of fringe benefit you'll have after the job is over."

She smiled at him. "You are the most surprising man," she said.

They waited at a corner for a traffic light to change, then walked on. "You said Colette believed us. Why? What did she say, Samantha?"

Sam felt the color rush to her cheeks, remembering what Colette had said about the way she looked at Derek, and how tender he was with her. Ridiculous. "Oh, uh . . . well, you heard her when she talked about people in love, the electricity in the air—all that romantic nonsense."

He stopped walking. "Is that what it is, Samantha? Romantic nonsense?" He looked down at her, his gaze probing.

"Well, you know," Sam said, gesturing with her hands, a habit of hers when she was flustered, "some of the things she said sounded unreal, like something out of a movie, or a romantic novel."

His eyes softened. "And you don't believe such feelings exist, do you, little one?" His hand brushed her cheek gently. "I hope someday you know that they do." He took a deep breath. "Anyway, we accomplished a good deal today. When we were leaving, Colette asked me if our engagement was to be kept secret. I told her we're getting married tomorrow, and she is free to shout it from the rooftops, if she wishes."

Sam grinned, relieved at the change of subject. "And will she?"

He smiled back. "Let me put it like this—Colette's

not a malicious gossip. If I had told her I wanted it kept quiet, she wouldn't have said a word to anyone. But now that I've indicated it's no secret—it just happens that one of her best friends writes a sort of combination society-gossip column, and Colette is one of her regular sources."

Sam shook her head. "Derek, you're unbelievable."

"Thank you," he said, casting his eyes down in a show of mock modesty. "It's simply a matter of knowing how to get things done. Speaking of which, here's a taxi."

At the hotel, he went into her room with her. At the connecting door he said, "I'd like to leave for dinner and dancing at eight. That gives you almost three hours. Will that be enough?"

Sam laughed. "I don't use so much makeup that it takes me three hours to put it on, Derek."

He smiled. "I can see that. But you look a little tired, and it'll be a late night. I thought you might want to take a nap. We can leave later than eight, if you like."

"No, eight is fine, Derek."

"All right, I'll see you then," he said, going into his room and closing the door. For a moment Sam stood looking at the door, her lower lip caught between her teeth, then she walked over and slowly, quietly, turned the lock.

She went into the bathroom and studied her face in the mirror. The fluorescent light showed purple smudges under her eyes, and her normally rosy cheeks were pale. Derek was right. She did look tired.

Sam decided to allow herself two hours for a nap. She undressed and lay down on the king-sized bed, and at once fell into a sleep disturbed only by dreams of Cinderella and a fairy godmother with shoe-button eyes.

She awoke before her alarm clock buzzed, feeling much refreshed. After a long, hot bath she was pleased to see that her eyes looked bright, the smudges having faded somewhat. She was still slightly paler than usual, but perhaps that was to be expected of a soon-to-be bride. She applied blush carefully, and began to look more like herself.

Sam took the last dress she had selected at Colette's carefully off the hanger. It was a deep purple chiffon, simply made, with a full skirt that seemed to float about her as she turned. A silver tie belt emphasized her tiny waist.

She was standing at the mirror, dabbing perfume behind her ears, when Derek tapped on the door. "Come in," she called. "I'm ready."

She realized her mistake almost as soon as the words were out, then she heard Derek's voice, tinged with irritation, "I can't come in, Samantha. The door's locked."

She hurried across the room, flustered, and opened the door. "I'm sorry. I forgot."

Annoyance vanished from his face as he looked at her. "You look lovely," he said. "That dress was a good choice." He seemed about to say something else, probably about the locked door, Sam thought with dread, but then shook his head and said, "Well, let's go. I'm starved."

They went to a restaurant at the top of one of the city's tallest buildings. Derek ordered for both of them. When the dinner was served—crisp green salad, steak, fresh mushrooms, and crusty, hot rolls— Sam found that she was famished, too.

From across the room a platinum-haired woman of about fifty fluttered her fingertips at Derek. He smiled and nodded. "That's Vivian Mason, the friend of Colette's I told you about. Look adoring," he said, grinning at her.

Sam smiled and batted her lashes. "Is this good enough, dear?" she simpered.

He chuckled. "If that's the best you can manage, Samantha, I guess I'll have to do the job of carrying off this charade myself." He took her hand and placed it against his lips. He opened her reluctant fingers and kissed her palm, tightening his hold on her wrist when she tried to pull back. "Keep smiling," he muttered through clenched teeth.

Sam forced the corners of her mouth upward in a travesty of a smile. It was the best she could do. The sensation of his lips kissing her hand was making her dizzy. Finally he released her wrist and gazed at her through half-lowered lids, the expression in his eyes unreadable. "Now *this* is what I mean when I say look adoring," he said. "You're doing better. Now you look like a woman who wants to be kissed, not one who's scared to death she may be."

Not knowing how to answer his outrageous remarks, confused by her own feelings, Sam took a sip of her wine. The orchestra began to play, and Derek said, "Come on, Samantha. It's time for the happy couple to dance for the photographers."

Sam stood, relieved that the tune was an old, romantic favorite. She had tried disco dancing once or twice and found it too frantic for her taste, much preferring the slow melodies of years ago.

When she turned into Derek's arms, he immediately pulled her much too close. She felt trapped in the vise of his embrace. She tried to back away from him, but he only looked down at her from his great height and grinned, his eyes full of the warning look she was coming to know so well. "It's all right, darling. We're engaged, remember?"

Sam resigned herself to finishing the dance in this uncomfortable closeness. She knew there was no way out of it, without creating a scene. It would serve him right if she did, though. Really, the man was so . . . overwhelming!

The music ended at last, and they found themselves by Vivian Mason's table. "Hello, Vivian," Derek said, wrapping an arm around Sam possessively.

"Derek, how are you? And is this the young lady Colette told me about? Of course, it must be. I'm Vivian Mason," she said, extending a many-ringed hand to Sam.

"Samantha Fielding," Sam answered.

"And I hear you two are being married tomorrow. Is that right?"

"Yes we are, Vivian," Derek said. "It was a sort of whirlwind courtship, wasn't it, darling?" he asked, hugging Sam, who could only manage a smiling nod. "We've known each other about four weeks," Derek went on, "but if I took my time, this one might get away from me, and I couldn't risk that."

They all laughed, and Derek went on to tell Vivian Mason that no, there was to be no press coverage of the wedding, but if she wished, they would pose for photographers here at the hotel, now. The words were hardly out before the lady had a phone at the table. A few minutes later, as Sam and Derek sat at their own table sipping champagne, a young man with a camera stood before them. Derek covered Sam's hands with his own as the flashbulb flared.

At the photographer's request, they returned to the dance floor, so he could get a few shots of them dancing. Sam didn't fight Derek this time, and he held her gently, moving in time to the music. She hardly noticed the flashbulbs, and didn't know the photographer had finished until Derek said, "You were very good, Sam. Thank you."

She looked up at him, touched by the sincerity in his voice. "Derek, I understand that you want people to think this is a real marriage, and I'm not prying into your reasons for that, but does it have to be this convincing? You're going to so much trouble to make our courtship seem genuine."

He hesitated. "Samantha, it's not that I don't trust you, but what you don't know you can't let out by accident. Trudy is the only one who knows—all I can tell you is that it *does* make a difference how good this looks. There are . . . people who might suspect that I married solely for legal reasons, and if they found out they were right, it would defeat my purpose. Those people are going to be skeptical when they hear about our marriage, so our conduct is going to have to bear close inspection."

Sam said, "Oh," not really understanding.

He smiled at her. "I don't mean to be mysterious, Samantha. You'll know the truth in time, and then you'll understand. To change the subject, did you know that dress turns those amazing eyes of yours the color of violets?"

Sam did indeed know that, it being the main reason for her choice, but she said sweetly, "Why, Derek, does it really?"

He laughed softly, his eyes warm, shaking his head. "Florida's answer to Scarlett O'Hara," he teased.

Sam joined him in laughter. "Well, we are in Atlanta, after all," she said. Now that she was more relaxed, it was surprising how good his arms felt around her. For the first time she found his strength comforting, rather than frightening.

"Speaking of which," he said, pulling her thoughts

46

back to their conversation, "how are you on Civil War history?"

"I love it. My dad used to tell me about the battles that were fought around Hollyville, and when we dug up our back yard for a garden we found several bullets from that time."

"Minie balls," Derek said.

"Yes. Oh, and a button with CSA, Confederate States of America, on the front. Dad was so excited he went out and bought a metal detector, but that was all he found on our land. He went out into the countryside and found quite a few relics though."

"I'd like to see those," Derek said. "Maybe I'll meet him someday."

Sam fell silent, suddenly thinking how much she *would* like her dad to meet Derek, and how unlikely that was.

"Well!" Derek said briskly, as if he had had the same thought. "The reason I brought the subject up is I thought you might want to play tourist tomorrow morning. Atlanta has a rich history. The wedding isn't until two o'clock, and we'll go straight from there to the airport for the flight to San Juan. So how about it? I can rent a car at the hotel."

Sam thought how odd it was for a bride to roam around the city reading historical markers on her wedding day. But this was not the usual sort of wedding day, and she would be glad to be busy, too busy to think.

"That sounds like fun," she answered, and then they were quiet, enjoying the music and the ease with which they danced together. It was as if they'd been doing this for years, Sam thought, closing her eyes and resting her head against Derek's chest. His hand tightened on hers slightly, as if in response, and his breath stirred her hair as he bent to her.

She felt his lips touch her temple gently, and stiffened in spite of herself, but this time it was Derek who drew back.

"We'd better go," he said quietly. "We have a big day planned tomorrow."

He was quiet in the cab back to the hotel. As before, he went into her room, then to the connecting door. Sam followed him, and stood with her hand on the knob, ready to close it behind him. He turned and put his hands on her shoulders.

"Good night, Derek," she said. "I enjoyed the dinner and dancing." She made her voice calm in spite of a tiny dart of fear that shot through her at the intensity of his gaze.

He shook his head. "It's no good, Samantha. We've got to talk about it," he said gently.

"About what?" she asked, conscious of the warmth of his hands on her shoulders.

He bent his head toward hers, and she drew back sharply. "About that," he said. "You can't keep tightening up every time I touch you. It'll give us away."

"That's ridiculous," she said, her voice low and furious. "No one can tell—"

"Believe me, Samantha, it shows. Am I such an ogre?" Not waiting for an answer, he pulled her to him with a suddenness that made her gasp. His head came down, his lips seeking hers. She tried to turn away, but he cupped her chin with a hand that seemed to be made of steel. His mouth smothered her protests.

Her struggles only served to wedge her more tightly between his arm and the unyielding strength of his chest, while he continued to kiss her as if he had all the time in the world, paying no attention to her attempts to free herself. She became acutely conscious of his firm, masculine body against her breasts, and her lips softened under his as waves of unfamiliar·feeling swept her. He released her chin, but she made no move to escape his kiss. Her arms, no longer pinned between them, circled his neck.

When he lifted his head from hers, she could only stare up at him, dazed. "That wasn't so terrible, was it?" he said, his voice husky.

Before she could find words, he bent once more and kissed her parted lips gently. Then he released her and stepped back, chuckling. "Good night, Samantha," he whispered, and closed the door behind him.

It opened again as Sam stood watching it, and Derek leaned into the room. This time his voice had an edge to it. "And leave this damn door unlocked. If I were going to rape you I'd have done it by now."

Four

When the door closed behind him once more, Sam felt her temper rising. The nerve of the man! She took a few steps toward the door, her hand outstretched to twist the lock sharply, but at the last moment she didn't dare. The thought of his anger was tempting, but also frightening.

She sat on the bed and unstrapped her high-heeled sandals, her head whirling with thoughts. That kiss—how could it have affected her so? She had never felt like that in Kyle's arms. If she had . . . she shook her head. It was just that Derek was so attractive, and he obviously had a great deal of experience with women.

Her mind kept returning to his kiss. It was as if she could still feel his lips pressed to hers. "That was not the kiss of a business partner, Sam," she muttered wryly.

It was the kiss of a man, she realized—a man who would not be satisfied forever with kisses. Would that be so awful? a traitorous voice inside her whispered. You *will* be married.

51

A harsh laugh tore from her throat. Married! Yes, but I won't—I *can't* endure a real marriage again. To go through what happened with Kyle again . . . She shivered, suddenly cold, and wished for the faded flannel bathrobe that still hung in the closet of her old bedroom at her father's house.

She took off the chiffon gown and put on her pajamas. She got into bed and lay wide-eyed, thinking of her girlhood home. It would be wonderful to be a child again, she thought, to be safe in her father's house. Maybe she ought to give up this idea and go back to Hollyville. She could get a job there, and take care of Dad. And Kyle wasn't there anymore; he was in prison, where he belonged.

As Sam thought about it her excitement grew. Why not? She knew her dad would be delighted. Of course she'd be letting Derek down, but . . . And there were all those clothes he'd bought today. But the only thing she'd worn was the chiffon gown. The rest could be returned. Still . . . she'd never gone back on her word before, and Derek would be furious, she knew. It was the thought of Derek's fury that decided her. She knew that his size and tremendous strength would make him dangerous in anger. And unstoppable in . . . love? No, lust, Sam thought, sickened as she remembered the acts that Kyle called love. No—never again!

She reached for the telephone beside her bed and dialed her father's number. It wasn't until he answered, his voice groggy with sleep, that she remembered how late it was.

"Dad, this is Sam. I'm so sorry, I forgot the time."

"Sam! Is everything all right? You're not hurt—"

"No, no. I'm fine. I just got a little homesick, and wanted to hear your voice."

She could hear his delight over the phone as,

reassured of her safety, he began to ask all about her new life in Florida. She decided to let him think she was calling from her apartment in Jacksonville Beach; it would save a lot of explanations.

For several minutes they chatted happily, bringing each other up to date. Sam was about to broach the purpose of her call when her father said, "Kyle's back in town, Sam."

She couldn't believe her ears. "What?"

"He's out on parole. I agreed to find a job for him. Of course, I couldn't take him back at the bank, but Joe Forman agreed to give him a chance in the accounting department down at his store."

"Daddy, how could you?" she cried. "After the things he did—"

"Now, Sam, he's changed. He was real poor as a boy, and I expect he got his values a little mixed up when he started handling all that money at the bank. But anyone can make a mistake, honey, and Kyle . . . well, he was like one of the family!"

"Oh, Dad," Sam moaned, covering her eyes with her free hand. She hated to hear that loyalty in his voice as he came to Kyle's defense. Kyle would only hurt him again, she knew.

"He's doing real good at his job, Sam. I can't say I feel the same about him as I used to, but I'm glad to see him get another chance."

"Dad, you be sure you don't forget what he did, though," Sam urged. "Don't trust him too much. There are things—" She stopped. It wouldn't serve any purpose to tell her father about her miserable marriage; it would only hurt him more.

"Well, to talk about more cheerful things, when are you coming home for a visit, Sam? Or better yet, moving back? You wouldn't have to see Kyle, honey. I know your marriage is over."

Sam brushed away a tear and made her voice cheerful. "As a matter of fact, it'll be some time before I can get home, Dad. I'm just starting a new job that I'm very excited about."

Sam bit her tongue as soon as the words were out. Her disappointment at realizing she couldn't go back to Hollyville—not while Kyle was there—had made her forget the nature of her new job.

"That's wonderful, Sam," her father was saying. "Tell me about it."

More lies, Sam thought miserably. "Well, Dad, I'm a . . . a public relations consultant for Spencer Industries. I'm going to be moving to a new place, so I'll call and give you my new phone number as soon as I'm settled."

"It sounds wonderful, honey. But you tell them you're going to need a vacation some time soon, so you can come home and visit your daddy, you hear?"

Sam ended the conversation as soon as she could, hating having to lie to her father. Her voice broke as she said, "I love you, Dad," and hung up. She lay back in bed, glad that she hadn't impulsively driven to Hollyville without calling. Anything was better than having to see Kyle again, even marriage to the fascinating, but frightening, man in the next room.

Derek had told her to dress casually for their sightseeing tour of Atlanta, and she put on yellow poplin slacks and was taking a terrycloth shirt with stripes of white and yellow from its hanger when she heard his knock on the door.

"Just a minute, I'm not dressed yet," she called somewhat frantically, remembering the unlocked door. In her haste to don the shirt, she caught a strand of her hair in one of its tiny decorative buttons. "Damn!" she said softly, and wondered where that had come from; she hardly ever cursed. Her anger was not appeased by the sound of quiet laughter through the door.

After a few moments of struggling with the shirt, she realized Derek was not going to burst into her room, and she was able to untwine her hair from the button. Taking her time, she stood before the mirror and combed it back into its customary neatness. Then she opened the door.

"Good morning, Samantha," he said, looking about the room. "Is there someone in here with you?"

"In here?" Sam asked, puzzled. "No, why?"

Now she could see the mocking light in his eyes, a corner of his smile turning downward. "Because I just heard a most unladylike word, and I'm sure it couldn't have come from those lovely lips of yours," he said, looking at her mouth.

"Oh! You—" She stopped, struck by the memory of his kisses last night, and found herself looking at the firmness of his chin, his lips . . . She forced her gaze back to his eyes, and the laughter in them. She made her voice cool. "Well, when one doesn't even have the privacy of a locked door . . ."

To escape his gaze, she turned and walked to the dressing table, applying blush she didn't need, certainly not at the moment.

He took a few steps to look over her shoulder into the mirror. "Now, Samantha, you know you're gilding the lily. You already look lovely."

"Thank you," she said shortly, tossing her lipstick, comb, and sunglasses into a straw tote bag to take with her.

"Will you listen to me?" he said, grinning, catching her hand to stop her busy work. "In a minute you'll start scrubbing the floor."

Sam had to laugh at her own transparency. "That would be awfully hard on the carpet, wouldn't it?"

"That's better," he said. "Now, you needn't worry about that unlocked door, Samantha. I'd be lying if I said I didn't find you . . . alluring, but there are easier and much more pleasant ways to enjoy . . . shall I say, feminine charms . . . than to charge into a lady's bedroom when she's dressing. It's much nicer to be invited in."

At first Sam found his words reassuring, then she felt an unexpected pang as she thought that a man as handsome as Derek must have been invited into many bedrooms. Before she could stop them, the words popped out. "I'm sure you would know all about that."

His eyes widened and he was quiet for a moment. Then the old mocking tone was back. "Why, Samantha, that sounded almost like a jealous wife. Could it be you're finally getting into the part?"

She turned so he couldn't see the color rushing into her cheeks. "Don't be ridiculous. Are you ready to go?"

Mercifully, he let the subject drop, but minutes later, in the hotel dining room, Sam found her thoughts returning to that conversation. Why on earth should she care about Derek's past conquests? Or present ones, for that matter? It was no concern of hers.

She pushed the troubling thought aside and concentrated on the menu. Derek insisted on ordering a hearty Southern breakfast for both of them—eggs, sausages, biscuits, and grits. As the waiter wrote on his pad, pretending not to listen, Derek said, "After all, today's our wedding day. You're going to need your strength!" The waiter's mouth twitched. Derek's eyes danced merrily, even when Sam gave him a sharp kick on the ankle.

Later Sam was glad she had had a big breakfast. Derek proved not to be a halfhearted tourist. In addition to the museums and well-known historical sites in the city, he took her out into the countryside to trace General Sherman's route into the beleaguered city. They climbed hills of red clay to survey Atlanta, as Derek pointed out where the retreating Confederate lines had stood. Listening to him, Sam could visualize the ragged ranks of old men and boys, striving gallantly to defend something that was already lost. Her interest was tempered with sorrow for rebel and Yank alike, in what seemed to her the saddest of all wars.

She looked up to find Derek watching her. He brushed a tear from her cheek and put an arm around her shoulder in silent understanding. Then they began the long descent to the rented car. When they came to a place where gravel made the path slippery, Derek took her hand. He kept holding it after the trail became smooth and straight, but Sam made no protest, enjoying the warm strength of his fingers entwined with hers.

When they reached the hotel again, Derek said, "Well, Samantha, I hate to rush a bride on her wedding day, but we have to be at Judge Norton's office in an hour. I thought we'd be back earlier."

His smile was kind, and Sam thought how warm his eyes were when he wasn't making fun of her. Aloud, she said, "It's all right, Derek. It's not as if it was a real wedding. I mean . . . well, you know."

"I know," he said, and it seemed to Sam that his voice was strangely sad. He must find deception as hard as she did, she thought. "Can you be ready in

57

forty-five minutes?" he asked. When she nodded, he left, closing the door.

Sam took a hasty shower. She noted with relief that the clothes from Colette's had arrived while she and Derek were out. She donned new lingerie, then sat at the dressing table to apply makeup. The smudges under her eyes were even more noticeable than yesterday. She sighed. Well, people will just have to think it's due to bridal nerves.

She slipped into the pink linen suit she had chosen for the wedding. With it she wore a silk blouse of deep rose that lent much-needed color to her pale cheeks. She transferred wallet and cosmetics to a white handbag and was ready, with fifteen minutes to spare.

Fifteen minutes to worry about whether she was making a terrible mistake. She laughed at herself in the mirror. Come off it, Sam! her reflection seemed to jeer. You worried for months about whether to marry Kyle, and you *still* made the wrong decision. Besides, this one doesn't even count.

She smiled ruefully as she wondered what the people back in Hollyville would say if they knew Sam Fielding was about to marry for the second time—a marriage she already knew was going to end in divorce! Thank goodness they didn't have to know.

There was a knock at the door, and Sam called, "Come in, Derek. I'm ready to go."

He wore a dark blue business suit, and looked exactly as he always did, but Sam's heart stopped for a moment as she looked at him and thought, He's going to be my husband—how handsome he is! Then the practical little voice inside jerked her back to reality. Come off it, Sam! it said, as it so often did.

For once, Derek seemed to feel awkward. "You

look wonderful," he said, then turned his glance away from her. He walked to the window. "I think we're going to have good weather for our flight."

"That's nice," Sam said weakly.

Derek stood at the window for several minutes, his back to her. She noticed he was beating his fist softly against the sill, in a kind of controlled anger.

Sam hesitated, then walked to him uncertainly. She reached up to touch his shoulder lightly. "Derek—?"

He turned, his eyes full of pain. "Dammit, it's the only way, but I feel—Sam, believe me, there's a good reason for this!"

It wasn't until they were in a cab, on the way to the judge's office, that she realized he had called her Sam.

Judge Norton turned out to be a little roly-poly Santa Claus of a man who had been a friend of Derek's father. His wife happened to be in the office when Sam and Derek arrived. She was a thin, stern-faced woman—until she smiled. Then she made a very appropriate Mrs. Claus. They both greeted Derek warmly. "I was downtown shopping," Mrs. Norton said, "and just stopped by to see Henry for a moment, but when he told me I had a chance to be a witness at the wedding of Tom Spencer's boy—well, I just had to wait."

The older couple beamed at Sam and Derek so happily that Sam felt guilty. She knew it must be even more difficult for Derek; these were his friends.

Judge Norton called his secretary to witness the ceremony also, and in moments Sam found herself standing beside Derek while the kindly old man began the wedding rites. Derek's arm braced her, and she knew it was because he could feel her trembling.

They repeated the vows woodenly. Sam wouldn't let herself think about the meaning of the words they said. When Judge Norton finally came to the end of the ceremony and said, "You may kiss the bride," Sam breathed a sigh of thankfulness that it was over. Derek bent down to her, and she could see the same pain in his eyes as before, in the hotel room. He kissed her briefly, perfunctorily, as if he no longer had the heart for their deception.

"You're going to have to do better than that, my boy!" Judge Norton laughed. "But then you have years together ahead of you. For now, let this old man steal a kiss from your lovely bride."

Sam felt tears sting her eyes as the judge kissed her smackingly on the cheek. Mrs. Norton hugged her. The secretary, a pretty girl of about eighteen, said breathlessly, "Oh, you're such a beautiful bride— and Mr. Spencer is so handsome! It's like a fairy-tale wedding."

Yes, Sam thought. Like Cinderella—only it's all a sham.

Derek's friends were all so kind to them; it made deceiving them all the more painful. Sam could see her own anxiety reflected on Derek's face and longed to comfort him. What would these nice people think of her if they knew she had entered into this deception for money? At least Derek had some compelling reason for his part in it. She felt her face burn with shame.

Derek glanced at her and read her feelings in her eyes. He told the Nortons they had to leave at once, that they were in a hurry to catch a plane. A few forced smiles at the newlywed jokes, and they were in a cab, headed back for the hotel. Derek said, "We'll have about thirty minutes to pack before we have to leave for the airport."

"I'll be ready," Sam answered tonelessly. After that they didn't speak for the rest of the trip.

In her room Sam slumped tiredly on the bed before Derek was through the door. He turned in the doorway and looked at her for a moment. "It's for a good reason, Samantha," he said softly. "It's worth it."

She nodded, not trusting her voice, and he left. She rose wearily and began packing.

Derek's spirits seemed to lift with the jet that carried them toward Puerto Rico. Sam felt her own mood lightening as well. If he said all of this was for a good reason, she believed that it was.

She knew Derek was really himself again when he began to tease her about a young couple who sat across the aisle one row ahead of them. "I'll bet they're newlyweds," he said, in a loud whisper. "I can always tell. See how they look at one another? Not like old married folks . . . not like us."

"Shh," Sam said, looking around to see if anyone had heard him. "You're impossible."

"No, really. See how he's holding her hand." Then he grabbed Sam's hand and put it to his cheek. He gazed at her with a smitten expression and sighed loudly, making such cow-eyes at her that she had to giggle.

The flight attendant arrived with their dinner trays and smiled down at them. "Here's your dinner, Mr. and Mrs. Spencer. You're newlyweds, aren't you?" she whispered. "I've gotten so I can always tell."

"Yes," Derek said in a strangled voice, "we are."

Sam leaned back in her seat, shaking with laughter. Soon Derek's chuckle joined hers. The flight attendant left, somewhat puzzled by the behavior of that nice couple, the Spencers.

Dinner included champagne. "Perfect," Derek said, "because this is a special day for us." He held his glass to Sam's, and for a moment she thought he was serious. "To you, Sam," he said softly.

He had called her Sam again! She opened her mouth to ask him why, but then the flight attendant returned with hot rolls. Derek made a great fuss over Sam for the girl's benefit—asking if she was comfortable, was her food all right, did she want a pillow. She saw the attendant smiling with wistful tolerance at Derek's display, and could have strangled him cheerfully. But all she could do was go along, and pretend to enjoy his solicitude.

When the girl left, Sam muttered, "Really, you are—are—"

"What?" he asked, grinning. "Wonderful? Gallant? Chivalrous?"

"Terrible."

"Why, Samantha, I'm crushed! Here I am, your new husband, my only interest the comfort and well-being of my little bride, and you show no appreciation at all—disgraceful," he said, shaking his head sadly.

"Terrible," she repeated firmly, then thought what a nice sound his chuckle was.

There was a limousine waiting for them at the airport in San Juan, and they were whisked to a hotel on the beach. As they walked into a lobby colorful with mosaic tile and lush plants, Sam felt a twinge of misgiving. After all, they *were* married this morning. She hoped Derek had no intention of trying to make this a real wedding night. No, he had made himself clear on that point in the beginning.

A tall, portly man with a handlebar mustache hurried across the lobby to greet them. "Mr. Spencer—

how good to see you again! I have reserved the bridal suite for you."

Sam felt her misgivings increase, then told herself sternly that he could hardly have asked for separate rooms on what was supposed to be his honeymoon, could he?

"Samantha, this is Raoul Delgado. He's another old friend of my father's, and the manager of the hotel."

They shook hands, and Señor Delgado called for a bellhop to take their luggage upstairs. He accompanied them to their suite to make sure it was satisfactory. When the bellhop had left, he said, "Again, my congratulations. And if there is anything you need, please call me."

As he closed the door, Derek gathered Sam into his arms. She knew it was so that Delgado, if he glanced back, would see the eagerness of a bridegroom, but then she heard the clicking sound of the lock catching, and Derek still held her. His mouth covered hers with an urgency that seemed born more of pain than of passion. She responded to his kiss, letting her lips move and open under his, knowing that this, at least, was no pretence.

He took his lips from hers and pressed them against her forehead, then stood still, holding her. "I've wanted to do that all day."

"Why, Derek?"

He laughed shortly, and moved back to look at her. "You are the most amazing woman. I don't think anyone else in the world would have had the perception to ask that question. They would assume they already knew the answer."

"But you haven't answered me," she said softly.

"Persistent, too, aren't you?" He sighed. "I think maybe you do know the answer, Samantha. Because, in the midst of all the lies we had to tell today, all the deception, you're the one person I can be honest with. And kissing you just now is the one honest thing I've done today. Do you understand that?"

"Yes. I felt the same way, about the dishonesty."

"And about the kiss, too?" he asked, only half teasing her.

"Yes," she whispered, afraid of where the word would lead.

For a long moment his blue eyes studied hers, then he reached for her hand. "Come on. Let's explore our territory."

They were in a large sitting room with an ankle-deep cocoa carpet. A sectional sofa covered in a nubby fabric of off-white angled around a large, low table of mahogany. Derek opened French doors leading to a wide balcony that faced the ocean. He smiled down at Sam. "I think we'll like it here, don't you?"

Sam nodded happily, and followed him back through the sitting room into the bedroom. It was decorated in gold and white, and also had French doors leading to the balcony. Sam tried to keep her eyes away from the king-sized bed, wondering how they were going to manage the sleeping arrangements. "Don't worry, Samantha. I'll sleep on the sofa," he said, grinning.

"Oh, but—" His habit of reading her thoughts was disconcerting.

An eyebrow arched as he said, mockingly, "Unless, of course, you insist—"

"No," she said hastily. "It just doesn't seem fair. I know—you sleep on the sofa tonight, and I'll take it tomorrow night."

He shook his head sadly. "And here I thought I was going to have to fight for my virtue."

"I don't think you'd fight very hard," Sam said dryly.

"You never know. Try me," he said, and bent down to her with his eyes closed, his lips puckered in an exaggerated fashion.

Sam giggled at the picture he presented. "No, thanks," she said, touching his lips with her fingers. "You obviously have a will of iron."

Laughing, he swooped her up in impossibly strong arms and spun them both about the room. "Oh, Samantha, Samantha!" Giving her a bear hug, he set her down, dizzy from the spinning. "I never expected this . . . business 'honeymoon' of ours to be fun, but . . . I like being here with you, Sam."

"Derek, you called—"

"Wait a minute," he said, pulling her by the hand back into the sitting room. "If I know Raoul Delgado—yes, here it is." On an intricately carved table against one wall stood a silver ice bucket containing a bottle of champagne, flanked by bowls of fresh fruit and tropical flowers.

"Let's change clothes and have some champagne," Derek said. "I'll dress out here. You can have the bedroom." He was loosening his tie as he spoke.

"All right," Sam said. He followed her into the bedroom to get his suitcase, then closed the door. She was glad to get out of the pink suit. She loved to travel, but it always made her feel grimy. After a moment's hesitation, Sam decided to take time for a quick shower.

The hot water made her feel relaxed and sleepy, and she suddenly realized what a long day it had been. Was it only this morning she had stood on a hill above Atlanta with Derek?

She pulled on brown slacks and a blouse of creamy satin with balloon sleeves. She drew a comb through her curls and decided she wasn't up to makeup tonight, instead satisfying her taste for feminine artifice by dabbing her favorite perfume behind each ear and on slender wrists.

She tapped on the door, and Derek said, "At last! I thought maybe you fell asleep," and opened the door. He wore blue jeans and a shirt of white silk, open part way down his chest. Sam could see the silver mat on his chest, the hair curling at the edge of his shirt, and drew her eyes away.

Derek poured champagne, and they carried their glasses out to the balcony. A soft breeze was coming off the ocean, stirring the palm trees, and a full moon bathed the surf in a glowing light. It was a beautiful scene, but as always, it was the sound of the ocean that moved Sam most. She closed her eyes and sighed peacefully, leaning on the balcony railing.

"Tranquil," Derek said quietly. "That's the word."

"Yes," Sam agreed. "Tranquil."

He touched his glass to hers. "To tranquility, and pleasant business associations."

Sam smiled, seeing in his words an attempt to reassure her, and sipped champagne.

"This is very different from my first wedding night," Derek said, as if remembering, and not happily.

"Mine too," Sam said, and couldn't stop the shudder that overtook her. Derek's eyes narrowed, watching her, and he was about to speak when Sam hurried on, to change the subject.

"What was Vicky like?" she blurted. Then, "Oh, Derek, I'm sorry. I know you weren't happy . . ."

"That's all right, Samantha. I guess neither of us has many good memories of our marriages, do we? Vicky was . . . well, when I married her, I thought it would last forever. Who doesn't? And when Debby was born, it was the icing on the cake." He stopped, shaking his head, and Sam thought he didn't want to talk about it anymore.

After a moment, though, he continued. "Only it seems Vicky wanted more than cake, more than Debby and me. I began to see sides of her I didn't particularly like fairly early in the marriage. She was grasping, very fond of material things, and unscrupulous. When I found out she had had a string of affairs beginning in the second year of our marriage, I finally got it through my thick skull that she had never loved me, but only the things I could buy for her. I was married to her for ten years, Samantha—ten years, and for eight of them she was unfaithful!"

He laughed ruefully and looked at Sam. "I guess that makes me pretty stupid, doesn't it?"

She touched his hand. "No, Derek, it makes you trusting. Because you're a good person, you thought she was too, that's all."

"What about you, Samantha?" he asked gently. "It's pretty apparent your marriage left you hurt."

"Yes," Sam said, and swallowed hard. "Kyle . . . Kyle stole money from my father's bank. He had been almost like . . . like a son to my father, even before we were married. He was like Vicky, in a way—he wanted a lot of material things. And he was unfaithful, too, but he didn't try to hide it. I think he wanted me to know." She stopped, her voice cracking. She took a deep breath. "Anyway, it's over now."

"There was more to it than that, wasn't there, Samantha?" he said softly. "That would account for anger, but not for the . . . fear I sense in you sometimes."

She looked away from him, eyes welling with unshed tears. "Yes, but I can't talk about it, Derek. I

. . . I just can't . . ." Her body shook with the effort to hold back a sob.

His arms folded around her, enveloping her in their warm safety. She laid her face against the cool silk of his shirt. "Shh, it's all right, little one. I shouldn't have questioned you." For a moment they stood together, Sam listening to the steady beat of his heart against her cheek, blending with the rhythm of the ocean. Then he set her back from him with a laugh.

"Now, Samantha, let's talk about happier things. It's almost football season. What do you want to bet the Gators will be the conference champions this year?" he asked, referring to the University of Florida's team.

Sam grinned, knowing he had gone to college in Gainesville. "Nope, I think Alabama will win it, as usual."

"Not after we beat Georgia, honey. Just wait. What do you say we go inside and have another glass of champagne?"

"All right. Derek—" she said, reaching for his hand.

"Yes?"

"Thank you for . . . the change of subject."

His eyes were soft in the moonlight. "You're welcome, little one."

They went inside and poured more champagne, then sank gratefully into the deep cushions of the sofa. When Derek slipped his arm around Sam's shoulder it seemed the most natural thing in the world, and she leaned against him, relaxing. He said, with a trace of his old humor, "Now all we need is a roaring fire to watch."

Sam giggled tiredly. "That would be a little warm for Puerto Rico, don't you think?"

"We could turn on the air conditioning."

Sam shook her head in mock rebuke. "Mr. Spencer, how wasteful! Besides," she added, looking around the room, "I'm not sure there is any."

"You hardly ever need it, right on the ocean," he said. "I have it at home, but I only use it a few days each year. The ocean breeze—you're going to love it, Sam. I can hardly wait to show you the beach. It's like it was made for you," he said.

The tone of his voice made Sam look up at him. "Samantha," he said, bringing his lips down to hers, and again it seemed completely natural. She raised her face to meet his kiss, touching her hand to the silver-gray stubble on his cheek.

His lips were gentle, coaxing her response. He lifted them from her mouth to touch light kisses to her closed eyes, to her throat. When he drew her to him more tightly and reclaimed her mouth, Sam could feel her heart thudding against his chest. Her hands moved upward until she could twine her fingers in the crisp curls at the nape of his neck. The tender pressure of his lips eased hers open, and she felt his tongue, tasting the sweetness of her mouth. She stiffened for the briefest of moments, then was swept along on a tide of sensations totally new to her.

He drew back to look at her. "My beautiful, beautiful Sam," he said, and she thought, This is the time I should leave, get out of here.

But then his mouth covered hers once more, and all thoughts were banished. There was only the dizzying touch of his lips, as they moved from her mouth to caress her ear, then trailed a line of kisses down her throat. His hand slid around from her back to cup her breast. A warning bell rang in her mind, but she ached for his touch in a way she had never thought possible. She felt his breath warm on her body as he slid the vee neck of her blouse aside to kiss the beginning swell of her breast. His hand stopped stroking her to work on the buttons of the blouse.

"Derek," she moaned, her hand slipping to the fastenings on his shirt. Suddenly she wanted nothing in the world as much as to feel his firm, matted chest against her breasts. Then they were planting soft, frantic kisses on one another, each struggling with buttons, each wanting the same fulfillment. Sam felt the cool air on her skin as Derek opened her blouse, touching her breasts through the lace of her bra, then began to unhook the back fastening.

"Damn these hooks," he muttered, and it was over. As soon as he said the words, Sam looked at him and saw Kyle, and a lacy bra that he had ripped brutally away from her body. "No! No!" she shouted.

Derek looked at her, his face white. "Samantha, what is it? Darling . . ." He tried to draw her into his arms.

She thrust herself backward, to the far end of the sofa, drawing her blouse together as if it were in shreds, not buttoning it, but holding it together. "Stay away from me," she said in a low voice, on the edge of hysteria. She began to shiver uncontrollably.

He went into the bedroom and came back in a moment with a bathrobe. It was his, and ridiculously big for her, but she snuggled into it and felt better, and when he handed her a snifter of brandy and told her to drink it, she looked up and saw, not Kyle, but Derek, and did as he said.

He sat on the part of the sofa that was at right angles to her. He leaned forward, elbows on knees, and watched her as she drank the brandy, taking the glass from her silently when she finished. When her eyes met his, she reddened, and said, "I'm sorry, Derek. I didn't mean . . ."

He cut her words off with a wave of his hand. "Never mind that. Are *you* all right, Sam?"

She nodded, drawing the robe more tightly about her. "I owe you an explana—"

Again he stopped her words. "You don't have to explain anything to me until you're ready to talk about it, little one—whether that's tonight, or tomorrow, or never. Do you think you could sleep now, or would you like to stay up for a while?"

She could see lines of tiredness and strain on Derek's face, and knew that she was exhausted, too. She stood. "I think I'll try to sleep. Oh, the robe—"

"You keep it, little one, if it helps. If I get cold maybe I'll wear one of those lacy numbers you got at Colette's."

That presented such a ludicrous picture that, tired as she was, Sam had to smile. "Good night, Derek."

"Good night, Sam."

But when Sam lay down between the satin sheets, sleep wouldn't come. She stared wide-eyed at the ceiling, while tears ran over her temples and dampened her hair. *It only proves what I should have known all along,* she thought. *I can never be a real wife to anyone.*

She reached for Derek's robe at the foot of the bed and put it on. The warm masculine scent of him was comforting, and at last Sam began to feel sleepy. Her last thought as she drifted off was that she had forgotten to ask him why he was calling her Sam at last.

Five

They had breakfast on the balcony the next morning, listening to the cries of seagulls overhead. Sam felt awkward with Derek, and was glad for the presence of the waiter. As for Derek, he was playing no games this morning; his solicitude for Sam was genuine.

When the waiter left them alone with their chilled melon and croissants, they ate in silence. Derek's mind seemed to be far away, and when he looked at Sam his eyes were grave.

As for Sam, she was full of regrets—regret that she hadn't met Derek first, before Kyle, and for what they might have shared, and now never could. And she was worried about what Derek might think after last night. She had let the nature of their relationship change. He had made it clear in the beginning that he expected only a business arrangement with her, and last night she had shown him a willingness to let it be more.

Now he would expect more, she thought miserably. And last night she had had to face reality: she had no more to give. As much as he attracted her, arousing in her feelings that astonished her with their intensity, there would always come a point where her arousal turned to terror, where Derek became Kyle.

She had to get their relationship back on its original footing. She stole a glance at him and found herself wanting to touch the crease in his brow, to smooth his frown away. She would have to steel herself against such feelings, remain detached.

He looked up to see her watching him, and smiled. "It's just as well we're going back tomorrow, Samantha," he said, stretching. "That sofa was definitely not meant to sleep on."

Sam stifled another pang of regret, that they had not shared the bedroom last night. "Derek, I . . . I have to talk to you."

He nodded. "Yes, Sam, what is it?"

Why did his calling her Sam make this more difficult? Her voice was cooler than she meant it to be as she spoke defensively. "When we made this . . . agreement, it was to be a purely business relationship. You made that quite clear."

"Yes," he said, and waited, watchfully.

"Well, I . . . I want it to stay that way."

"What exactly do you mean by that?" She could hear the control in his voice. Why was he making her go on and on about this? He knew what she meant.

"I . . . I don't want . . . you touching me, kissing me!" she blurted, starting to rise.

His hand shot out and captured her wrists across the table, forcing her back down in her chair. He leaned across the glass surface, upsetting his coffee. His eyes were dark as they held her own, and Sam could read something like pain in them. "Now listen to me," he said, his voice coming low through clenched teeth. "I kissed you, and touched you, yes. But only when the signals I got from you said full speed ahead!"

She turned her face away from him, reddening. His hand pulled her back to look at him. "As soon as those signals changed, I respected them, which is not the easiest thing in the world, for your information!" His voice softened. "Do you think I need a woman so badly that I would . . . rape a frightened child? Because that's what you became last night, Sam. You have nothing to fear from me."

Voice trembling, she said, "Then you will . . . leave me alone?"

His tone harshened once more. "Dammit, what did I just say? Now listen, Sam," he said, his grip tightening painfully on her wrist, "when we're around people, particularly back in Jacksonville, I'll have to kiss you occasionally, and put my arm around you. But don't worry," he added, a mocking light in his eyes, "I don't think I'll enjoy it any more than you will. And when no one's around, I won't bother you."

He left the balcony. Sam sat at the table, looking at the puddle of coffee through shimmering tears. She had done what she meant to do, so why did she feel so miserable?

She brushed the tears away hastily as Derek spoke from behind her. "Would you like to go shopping in Old San Juan? Then this afternoon we could go swimming."

"If that's what you'd like," she said.

He shrugged. "It's what would be expected of newlyweds here for the weekend."

The contrast between his apathy and yesterday's exuberance, when he had swung her around the room, made the tears start anew. "All right," she said, turning so he wouldn't see her face. "I'll go get ready."

Remembering the heat of the sun on the balcony, she wore white walking shorts and a lightweight top of blue cotton. Derek wore white slacks and a madras shirt. As they walked through the lobby, Señor Delgado hailed them.

"Good morning," Derek said, slipping an arm around Sam's shoulders. She tried not to stiffen, but found it as difficult as it had been in the very beginning of this strange relationship.

"I have some mail for you," the older man said. "I trust your suite is satisfactory?" he asked, smiling.

"Yes, very. Well, good morning." Sam thought even Señor Delgado must notice the difference between Derek this morning and the boisterous young man of yesterday.

Derek leafed through the mail as they walked toward the hotel entrance. "Here's one for you, Samantha," he said, handing her an envelope. It was her first salary check. "It should have been here yesterday," Derek said. "Spencer Industries pays on Fridays."

She slipped the check into her tote bag wordlessly, thinking how much things had changed since she had agreed to take this job.

They spent the morning walking through the narrow streets of Old San Juan, stopping to browse in the small shops along the way. Sam spent most of her first paycheck on a beautifully carved chess set of teak and ivory, a gift for her father. It cost more than she could afford, and she knew it was a sop to her conscience for all the lies she had told her father, and the lies she would have to tell him in the next months.

They returned to the hotel for a light lunch neither tasted, then went upstairs to change into bathing suits. Sam frowned as she looked at her reflection, wearing the abbreviated pink bikini Colette had persuaded her to take. It looked even skimpier now than it had at the shop.

She sighed. It was the only swimsuit she had with her, so there was nothing to do but slip on the pink terrycloth beach coat that came with it, and be grateful she was slim. She knew she looked good in the suit, but had the feeling it would be disastrous to try to swim in it.

When at last they were on the beach Derek looked at her questioningly for a moment, then said he was going for a swim. For a few moments she simply sat in the bright sun, then decided, this is ridiculous, and took off the concealing robe. She lay on her stomach, enjoying the feeling of warmth on her back, the soothing sound of the ocean almost lulling her to sleep.

She woke to hear Derek chuckling, with a trace of the old warmth in his voice. "I see why you didn't want to go in the water. You're a cautious woman, Sam."

She turned over and looked up at him. He seemed to tower over her, standing there. She tried not to look at his body, the chest matted with silver hair, the strongly muscled legs—the body she had wanted last night with a hunger that for a time made her forget her fear.

He lay down on the chaise next to hers, eyes closed, enjoying the sun as she did herself.

She relaxed and lay back down. Derek said, "I thought I'd better come out of the water and make sure you hadn't fallen asleep in the sun, but I needn't have worried. You're not going to burn easily."

"No," she said. "I never burn easily. My skin is naturally dark."

"Yes," Derek said, "like mine."

"Mmm," Sam murmured, enjoying the feeling of . . . well, almost anonymity in talking like this, with their eyes closed. It was easier to talk to Derek without his penetrating, sometimes mocking gaze on her. "My mother was part Spanish," she said, "and I inherited her coloring."

"She's not living, is she, Sam?"

"No, she died when I was a baby."

"That must have made things hard for you," he said gently.

She thought for a moment. "There were times when I missed her, missed having a mother, and I wish I had been old enough to remember her. But Dad . . . well, he's been wonderful to me, always."

They were silent for a moment, listening to the peaceful sounds of the ocean and the seagulls. "What about you, Derek? Did Colette say your mother passed away two years ago?"

"Yes, she did."

"And then your father last year. To lose both of them in such a short time—that must have been awful for you."

For a moment he didn't answer. "Well, Dad . . . Dad died a little with Mom. He seemed lost without her. I guess that's why it seemed so important to him that Vicky and I . . ." His voice trailed off.

Sam tried to think of something to say to ease his pain, wondering how he would blame himself for his father's death, for Vicky's destructiveness.

"Your father sounds like an interesting man, Sam, from the things you've told me about him."

"I guess he is. All I know is he's a very good man,

78

and a wonderful father. I don't know what I would have done without him when Kyle—" She stopped.

"Kyle made you think it was all your fault, didn't he?" he asked abruptly. Sam opened her eyes to find he had sat up and was watching her face. She drew an arm up to shield her eyes from the sun, and looked at him from under it.

"Yes, he did. How did you know?"

"Because Vicky had the same knack," he said, his eyes full of remembered pain. "No matter how many rotten things she did, she managed to twist the facts until I became the villain. The sad part is, for a long time I believed her."

"I guess we look for reasons," Sam said, considering. "When someone does something to hurt us, we wonder if we caused it."

"You shouldn't, Sam. Your marriage obviously left deep scars, and I'll bet your husband—your ex-husband is pretty much the same as the day you married him. It took me a while, but I finally learned there are some people who are just . . . bad. You can't let them go on hurting you forever." He laughed shortly and lay down once more. "Oh, well, that's enough preaching for one day," he said.

Sam thought about his words, lying there relishing the sun's warm rays. It's true, she thought, Kyle was bad, wicked—she knew that. But maybe Kyle *would* go on hurting her forever, as he had hurt her last night.

They had a leisurely dinner of lobster in the hotel dining room, then walked along the terrace in the moonlight. Inside the orchestra played soft music. The palm trees were silhouetted blackly against the moonlit beach, and there were several couples on the terrace, enjoying the romantic setting.

Suddenly Derek bent and kissed her. As she started to draw back involuntarily, he whispered, "There's Delgado," and she let herself be drawn into his arms. He kissed her woodenly, his mouth closed, lips still. When he released her, she saw Señor Delgado leaving the terrace. Sam realized with a shock that she had thought—no, she had *hoped*—Derek was lying to her, as an excuse to kiss her.

The kiss itself should have destroyed that illusion, she told herself miserably. What was the matter with her? He was giving her exactly what she insisted on so forcefully this morning.

When they returned to the room, neither could find much to say. Sam knew they were both remembering the night before. Finally Sam said, "I'm tired, Derek. If you don't mind, I think I'll go to bed."

She got a blanket and began to make up the sofa.

"I'll sleep on the sofa," he said.

"No. You slept here last night."

"Sam, don't be ridiculous," he said, taking the blanket from her.

She turned and faced him. "Look, Derek, fair is fair. Besides, I'm a lot shorter than you are. It will be more comfortable for me."

When she continued to insist he shrugged. "All right. See you in the morning," he said, and went into the bedroom.

After she finished preparing the sofa she realized she was still wearing the dress she wore at dinner, and all her things were in the bedroom. Rather than disturb Derek, she decided to sleep in her bra and panties.

She tossed about restlessly for some time, the wool blanket making her skin itch. She sat up as she heard the bedroom door open. "Derek? What—"

"Come on," he said briskly. "I want you to take the bedroom."

The direction of his glance in the moon-bright room made her aware that the blanket had fallen to her waist. She pulled it up, wrapping it around her. "No, I said I would sleep on the sofa tonight, Derek."

"Come here," he said, grasping her hand. She had to choose between freeing herself or holding onto the blanket, so she followed him meekly into the bedroom. "Here," he said, thrusting a pillow at her. "Smell this."

"What—?" Puzzled, she put her face against the pillow, and smelled her favorite perfume, the scent she had worn the night before.

"If you want to continue to sleep in safety," he said tauntingly, "I suggest you give me my trusty old sofa back. All right? Unless you're *trying* to drive me wild."

She smiled. At least she could put on something more comfortable to sleep in now. "All right, Derek. Thank you."

Alone in the room she smiled again. It was nice to have him teasing her again, talking to her in that especially warm tone he used sometimes.

She decided that a hot bath might help her sleep, and soaked for a while in the steamy tub. She did feel more relaxed, and looked forward, if somewhat guiltily, to sleeping in the bed. Derek was right—the sofa *was* uncomfortable.

Sam dried with a fluffy towel and drew on a pair of pink panties with wide lace borders. Then she donned one of her favorite sleeping garments, a football jersey that had been a gift from a suitor in her high school years. It swallowed her tiny frame, hanging almost to her knees.

She slipped between the sheets. She smelled the

perfume on the pillow again, and wondered if it had really driven Derek wild, as he said, or if that had been a cover for his chivalrous gesture. She fell asleep smiling.

Sam knew she was dreaming, but at the same time it was real. She and Derek were dancing together, but they were on the beach. She was wearing a beach coat that kept turning into her gown of purple chiffon, streaming about her as she whirled in Derek's arms. He kissed her, and this time she felt no fear, answering his kisses eagerly, with unafraid innocence. He touched her and she wanted him. She loved him and wanted to know all his love. He drew her down on the sand, the weight of his body atop her. "Yes, Derek, yes . . ." she moaned.

"Open your eyes, darling," he said, and there was something strange about his voice. She looked up at him and it was Kyle, smiling cruelly.

"No, no!" she screamed. "Kyle, please let me go! Haven't you hurt me enough?" She struggled wildly, but his arms held her like steel bands, crushing her. She screamed again and again as he laughed at her helplessness, possessing her brutally. "Wake up, Sam. It's all your own fault, because you're frigid! Wake up . . ."

She opened her eyes. Derek was shaking her gently, saying, "Wake up, Sam, wake up. It's only a nightmare, little one."

She threw her arms about his neck and sobbed, clinging to his warm strength as if she would never be safe again. "Derek, it was awful, awful . . ."

"Shh, it's all right," he crooned, picking her up in his arms like a child, rocking her. "It's all right." He sat on the edge of the bed, holding her, and she was afraid to let him go.

She buried her face against his robe and sobbed. He stroked her hair and said, "It's all right, little one. I won't let anyone hurt you, little Sam. Shh," he whispered.

It was a long while before her sobs subsided, and she was able to turn her mind away from the horror of her nightmare.

"I'm sorry I woke you, Derek," she said, her voice hoarse.

"Don't be silly," he murmured against the top of her head.

She sighed. "They're going to throw us out of this hotel if I yell anymore." She felt his great chest shake with laughter.

"Yes, I really think you should stop, Sam," he chuckled. "You must be feeling better, if you're starting to worry about what the neighbors will think."

She nestled closer against him and drew a deep, shuddering breath, feeling a comfort in his warm nearness that she didn't want to examine too closely, not just now.

"Derek," she whispered, "why do you call me Sam now? I thought you weren't going to."

Now he laughed in earnest, not answering her.

"Come on, Derek. Why?" she said more insistently.

Through his laughter, he said, "All right, all right. I changed my mind, that's all. Because I was wrong about you—you *are* a Sam."

"Oh," she said. She sat in his arms silently for a moment, then raised her head to look at him. "And what is *that* supposed to mean?" she asked, with some heat. .

He raised his brows in mock innocence. "You're

hard to please, aren't you? I thought you *wanted* to be called Sam."

"I do, but—"

"What I mean, little one, is that to me it seemed unusual to call a woman Sam, while Samantha was an ordinary feminine name. Sam just didn't fit the pattern. Only it suits you, because you don't fit any pattern I've ever seen. You are absolutely unique."

Sam considered his words for a moment. "That's not necessarily good," she said doubtfully.

She felt his chest shake with laughter once more, and looked up at him. His blue eyes were dancing. "You *are* going to drag it out of me, aren't you?" he said. "All right, *Sam,* you are the most fascinating, temptingly feminine bundle of contrasts I've ever known—from the top of your charming curls, to that godawful football jersey, to those fetching lacy panties—"

Sam realized the football jersey had pulled up around her waist in her nightmare struggles, and hastily tugged it down.

He chuckled and continued, "—not to mention your swings from little girl wanting to be comforted to proper young woman who must keep her skirt down. Now, do you think you've recovered sufficiently to be able to sleep?"

"Yes," she said, suddenly embarrassed to be sitting in his lap. She struggled to stand up, aware of his maddening chuckle as she did so. He rose from the bed and made a bow of mock gallantry. "If my services are no longer required, I think I'll retire . . ."

"Good night," she said. Then when he was at the door, "Derek?" He turned. Childlike once more, timorously, she said, "Would you leave the door open, please?"

His face softened as he nodded.

Once in the night she heard him snoring. It seemed strange to think of Derek Spencer, always so in control of himself, snoring, but Sam thought it was the most comforting sound she had ever heard, as reassuring as the constant din of the surf.

Six

Their flight left early the next morning. Tired from the restless night, Sam slept most of the way. Once settled in Derek's Mercedes, she found herself dozing off again, in spite of herself. She woke when the car stopped, in front of her old apartment.

"Wh—what are we doing here?" she asked groggily.

Derek smiled at her. "I believe there's something you wanted to pick up here, sleepyhead."

"Tiptoe!" Sam exclaimed, suddenly eager to see her cat. She scurried out of the car. Derek walked with her to Mrs. Hotchkiss's apartment.

The landlady opened the door, beaming. "Miss Fielding! Or I guess I should say Mrs. Spencer—I was just reading about you," she said, brandishing a newspaper. "Come in, come in. And this must be Mr. Spencer?"

"Yes," Derek said, extending a hand. "So the Jacksonville papers have the story already, do they?" He sounded pleased.

"Oh, they're full of the news, Mr. Spencer—the

wedding, shopping, a trip to Puerto Rico—it's all so romantic!" she said. "And the pictures—you two make such a lovely couple."

Sam and Derek were murmuring thanks when she noticed an insistent, recurring pressure against her ankle and looked down to see Tiptoe, walking back and forth, leaning against her. She bent and picked him up, his purring growing louder as she did.

She could tell he had missed her, for he launched into what was for him an absolute frenzy of affection—butting his head against her cheek, flexing and clenching his paws, and letting himself be held for minutes without asserting his independence by leaping out of her arms. He went so far as to tolerate Derek's touch—since the stranger knew the right spot to scratch under a cat's ear—although he half-opened his eyes as a signal that he was perfectly aware this was not his owner's hand.

Mrs. Hotchkiss frowned, looking at the newspapers. "There's one thing I don't understand, Miss Field—Mrs. Spencer," she said. "These stories all say you're from Atlanta, and not one word about you living here in town. Why on earth did they make a mistake like that?"

Derek answered. "You see, Mrs. Hotchkiss, people in my position sometimes have trouble getting any privacy, and I didn't want the press hounding Sam—or you. So we decided to be married in Atlanta, and let it be thought that was Sam's home. I'd appreciate it if you'd help us keep that secret," he said smoothly.

The story sounded thin to Sam, but Mrs. Hotchkiss seemed to love the intrigue, and nodded wisely. "I won't say a word, Mr. Spencer. Oh, it's all so romantic," she breathed, eyes shining. "Oh! Mrs. Spencer—your father's been trying to reach you."

"Dad? Is anything wrong?" Sam asked, suddenly sure that he was ill. *It's because I feel guilty about the lies, he's in good health,* her mind babbled.

"No, I think he heard about your marriage," Mrs. Hotchkiss said uncomfortably. "He asked me some questions, but of course I didn't know that much—"

"I'd better call him—"

"Sam, I have a key to Ned's apartment. You can call from there." He smiled at Mrs. Hotchkiss. "Mr. Palmer is my attorney. He won't mind."

Sam hardly heard the landlady's good wishes, barely remembering to thank her for keeping Tiptoe, she was so upset about her father. Now she had to call and tell him more lies.

Even forewarned as she was, Sam winced at the pain in her father's voice. He had read about her marriage in the newspapers. "What was it, Sam— were you afraid to tell me? Afraid that I still wanted you and Kyle—"

"No," Sam broke in. "Dad—please forgive me. It . . . it was just so . . . everything happened so fast . . ." She looked at Derek as if he could help her. She could see the sympathy in his eyes, but knew he couldn't do this for her.

Her father sighed. "Well, I guess the only important thing is—do you love him, Sam?"

She hesitated. All the lies—it was too much. She caught Derek's eyes once more, filled with understanding. Of course he understood; he had gone through the same thing with his friends—but this was her *father*. Still, she had entered into an agreement with Derek . . .

"Yes, Dad, I do. I wouldn't have married him otherwise."

"What's he like, Sam?"

"Well," she answered, acutely conscious of Derek standing beside her, "he's intelligent . . . tall . . . very attractive—" She stopped, knowing her voice was about to break. I can't do this, she thought desperately, tears beginning to streak her cheeks. When Derek reached a hand for the telephone, she gave it to him willingly.

"Mr. Fielding? Derek Spencer," he said cordially.

Sam moved away from the phone, so her father couldn't hear her weeping. Derek looked at her as he spoke. "Yes, sir, very much. No, we haven't known each other very long."

Sam dried her eyes, listening to Derek's side of the conversation. She hoped he could comfort her father, but then, when this marriage broke up—well, perhaps she would be able to tell him the truth then.

Derek was looking at her again, his eyes grave. "Yes, sir, I know she is. Very special. I will." A few seconds later he extended the phone to Sam. "Your father wants to speak to you, Sam."

Woodenly she took the instrument. "Yes, Dad?"

"He sounds like a nice young man, Sam. Bring him back here for a visit soon, won't you?"

"Yes, Dad. I . . . I'll try."

"Are you okay, honey? You sound a little shaky."

"We . . . we had an early flight this morning, and, well, as I said, everything's been happening so quickly . . . I guess I'm a little tired."

He seemed to accept Sam's explanation, and after a few minutes it was over. She replaced the receiver and stood still, arms hanging limply by her sides, eyes staring dully ahead into space.

So many lies, she thought tiredly. First her marriage to Kyle, pretending constantly that they were happy. Now this. Her whole adult life had been a lie . . .

Derek saw the pain in her face and reached out to comfort her, drawing her into his arms. She recoiled, thrusting herself away from him. Her vehemence caught them both by surprise as she burst out, "Is there an audience now, Derek? Are you trying to convince someone this marriage is the real thing? We both know it's phony, like all the other lies—so if there's no one here but us, leave me alone!"

His face went white, his eyes darkening as he stared at her. "You won't have to tell me again," he said coldly.

Sam felt a door had closed between them. For a moment she wished she could recall her words, but it was too late.

Derek went on, his voice harsh, "Just make sure you control your revulsion when we're in public. Now get your cat and we'll go home, *Mrs.* Spencer."

Tiptoe made himself comfortable in the rear window of the Mercedes. Sam stared at the scenery through tear-filled eyes as Derek drove northward along the coast.

The silence felt heavy in the air between them. Why did I lash out at him? Sam thought miserably. I don't want it to be like this.

In an effort to break the quiet, she said, "Your daughter—Debby—will she be there?"

"No. She's with Vicky's parents. She'll be . . . coming home next week."

Something in his tone made Sam long to ask him more about his daughter. "I guess you'll be glad when she's back, won't you?"

He glanced at her, then back at the road. "You

needn't make conversation," he said shortly. "We're alone."

She turned her face to the window to hide the pain she was sure showed in her eyes. Is this the way things were going to be between them from now on? she wondered. Well, it was *your* decision, Sam, she told herself sternly.

The Mercedes turned off the main highway onto an oyster shell road. They came to the top of a small hill with the sound of the ocean close at hand. Before them lay Derek's home—a white stucco villa with a red-tiled roof. The car eased into a courtyard vibrant with flowers.

Sam got out and reached into the back for Tiptoe, then looked around her. "Derek, it's beautiful."

For a moment it seemed his face softened once more as he watched her. Then a plump, gray-haired woman came out through the arched doorway of the villa, followed by a dark young man. "Mr. Derek, it's good to have you home."

Sam was introduced to Mrs. Holmes, the housekeeper, and the young man, who was her grandson Phillip. They all talked for a few moments, then Derek said, "Phillip, if you'll get our bags out of the car, I'd like to show Mrs. Spencer around."

He took Sam's arm and escorted her into her new home. They walked through a wide hallway into a vast, sunken living room. Thick white shag carpet covered the floor, and the sofas and chairs were deep, made for comfort. One wall was covered with books, leatherbound classics mingling freely on the shelves with brightly jacketed modern novels and well-worn paperbacks. Derek's library didn't look orderly; it looked enjoyed.

Gesturing to the right, Derek said, "Over there are the dining room, a breakfast nook, and the kitchen.

You'll see those later. This way," he said, guiding her toward the left, "to our rooms."

As they walked down the long hallway, Derek nodded toward a door on his left. "Guest bathroom." Then the next door on the left. "Debby's bedroom and bath through there." Then across the hall, he walked into a room, turning to her. "This is the master bedroom. I've used it for years. I trust you won't think I'm unchivalrous if I keep it." A trace of the old mockery was in his voice. Sam found even that a welcome change from his coolness earlier.

"That seems reasonable," she said sweetly. "Where do I sleep?"

His mouth twitched, and for a moment the laughter reached his eyes. He sighed heavily. "Ah, well, if you insist on sleeping alone—" He led her to a door from his room through a dressing room, into a spacious bedroom. Here the carpet was a dusty rose shade of plush. The bedspread and draperies were cream, trimmed in a deeper rose. Sliding glass doors led to a terrace and beyond, to the ocean.

"You have your own bath, through there," Derek said, indicating the far wall. "And you can have the dressing room."

"Derek, it's lovely," Sam said, opening the glass doors, letting the sound of the Atlantic drift inside. Tiptoe, who had been following them from room to room, found this more to his liking. He curled up in a sunny spot on the terrace for a nap.

Derek laughed. "That looks like a good idea. If you'd like to nap for a while, I'll show you the rest of the place later," he said. A host being polite to a guest, Sam thought with a pang. But at the door he turned and said softly, "I really *am* looking forward to showing you the beach, Sam."

As soon as she was alone, Sam realized how tired

she was. She lay down on the bed and fell asleep almost immediately. A soft breeze caressed her face, the ocean whispered its lullaby, and Derek was nearby. In the vulnerability of exhaustion she didn't question this last point—she only knew it was good.

When she woke it was late afternoon. She hurried through a shower, anxious to see the beach before dark. Her bathroom proved to be quite luxurious, with a huge sunken marble tub as well as the shower stall, and she promised herself a long bubble bath later. She pulled on white shorts and a pink terrycloth top and combed her hair quickly. She looked so refreshed after her nap, her cheeks blooming with good health, that she decided to skip makeup.

She walked down the hallway through the living room, but there was no sign of Derek. She found Mrs. Holmes in the kitchen preparing dinner. "I think Mr. Derek's on the terrace. I believe he's talking things over with that cat of yours," she said, eyes twinkling.

He was indeed. Sam found Derek stretched out on a lounge chair. And stretched out on Derek, right across the knees of his immaculately pressed trousers, was Tiptoe, paws flexing in admiration of this new person who knew how to behave with a cat.

Derek looked up when Sam joined him on the terrace. "I think Tiptoe's going to be able to adjust to life here, Sam," he said, grinning. "I was just about to take him in to Mrs. Holmes for some dinner. Then you and I can walk on the beach."

A few minutes later Derek returned from the kitchen to lead Sam down a well-worn path to the beach. They walked along the water's edge barefoot, letting the surf wash over their feet and ankles.

The coastline curved outward to embrace a natural harbor. In the distance Sam could see the line of a creek extending inland. "What is that, Derek?" she asked, pointing ahead.

"Pirate's Creek," he said. "At least that's what the neighborhood kids called it when I was growing up. We used to say Blackbeard buried treasure there."

"Did you ever look for it?" she asked with a grin.

He laughed. "As a matter of fact, yes. When we were kids we used to go up there, frightening each other with tales of Blackbeard's ghost all the way. And one summer a bunch of us—teenagers by then—took shovels and metal detectors and went looking in earnest."

"Did you find anything?" she asked hopefully.

He glanced at her, eyes shining with laughter. "About every mosquito in the country. But it was the water moccasin that made us decide to let Blackbeard's ghost keep his treasure."

She smiled, and for a while they walked in companionable silence. How strange to realize she'd known this man—why, tomorrow would be a week! It seemed as if she'd *always* known him. What was there about him? It was almost as if—

"Penny for your thoughts."

Sam looked up, startled. "I was just thinking it seems as if I've known you much longer than a week."

Something crossed his face and was gone. He took a step toward her, then stopped. "Come on, Sam," he said, smiling gently. "Let's get back to the house. Mrs. Holmes will have dinner ready."

Since the afternoon had been so hot, Mrs. Holmes had fixed them a cold supper of chicken salad, fresh fruit, and chilled white wine. After they ate, Derek put their coffee cups on a tray and led Sam to a screened porch overlooking the beach. It was bright with white wicker furniture and large potted plants, a cheerful place. She wasn't surprised to find Tiptoe had already discovered it. It was his favorite kind of spot for sleeping. He was stretched out in the only armchair, forcing Derek and Sam to share the wicker love seat.

They sat close together, enjoying their coffee in the twilight, listening to the tide coming in. Once again Sam felt a pang of wistfulness—it would be nice if this were real. But for her—no, it could never be.

Sam slept deeply that night, with no nightmares, lulled by the familiar sound of the Atlantic. She had closed the door between her room and Derek's, but had not locked it.

When she woke the next morning she was disappointed to learn from Mrs. Holmes that Derek had already left for the office. She had a light breakfast of grapefruit and coffee, then walked along the beach collecting shells. In the afternoon she unpacked the things that had been sent from her apartment, then wandered about disconsolately, looking at her wrist-watch frequently.

At home when she was in this frame of mind, she would tackle some long overdue cleaning job, but here a cleaning woman came in daily to help Mrs. Holmes clean the already sparkling house. Sam went out to the terrace and sat down. Tiptoe jumped on her lap and bathed his paws, preparing for a nap. Well, at least I'm good for *something*, Sam thought. Never mind, next week Debby will be here. I can spend my time getting to know her.

Sam was surprised at the long hours Derek spent at the office. She realized she had been thinking of him as a sort of playboy executive in an inherited family business, and felt guilty for having misjudged him. Unless he's *not* at the office, she thought, and wished it hadn't occurred to her. What business was it of hers? something inside her taunted. Was she feeling like a jealous wife? This was a *business* arrangement, remember?

Tuesday dragged on interminably, as Monday had done. When Derek came home it was after dark, and they had just sat down to dinner when the phone rang. Sam answered it. Gloria, in honeyed tones, asked to speak to Derek. He spoke with her briefly, then returned to the table.

"I've got to go out after dinner," he told Sam. "A business emergency."

Sam nodded, sure he was lying—but she had no right to question him. She was his employee, not his wife. She shouldn't *care.*

"Oh, by the way," Derek said, "Trudy's coming for dinner tomorrow night."

"Wonderful," Sam answered. "I'll look forward to seeing her."

"You two really hit it off, didn't you?" Derek asked, smiling. "That figures."

Sam set her coffee cup down. "Now, Derek, what does that mean?"

"You really pick at things, don't you? Why don't you just assume it's complimentary? After all, I adore Trudy." His eyes had that glint that always made Sam feel he could read her mind.

"It's the way you put things—" Sam said, exasperated. "It always makes me wonder—"

He laughed. "In some ways you two are alike, that's what I meant. She can't stand phonies, either."

Sam laughed shortly. "I don't see why she likes me, then. I feel like the biggest phony in the world!"

Derek, his eyes riveted to hers, spoke so softly she

had to lean across the table to hear his words. "There's nothing phony about you, Sam. If there were, this . . . situation would be easier for you. And, remember, Trudy knows about our arrangement."

Sam nodded. "Yes. It'll be a relief to talk to someone I don't have to . . . pretend with."

Derek frowned. "Speaking of pretending, our trial by fire will be coming up this weekend—the office picnic. The company has a cottage on the beach, and once a year we have a big party there—a cookout, swimming, dancing—the works. We have to go, Sam, and we have to put on a good act."

Sam's eyes widened. "That sounds scary, Derek, almost as if . . . we're being judged or something."

He laughed. "Well, it's not quite that bad. But I am the president of the company, and they all know we just got married, so they'll be curious about us." His face darkened. "And someone there may be more than a little curious. It's important that we come across as the genuine article, a happy couple who just got married."

"I'll do my best, Derek," Sam said. He left a few minutes later. At eleven o'clock when Sam went to her bedroom, he hadn't returned. She was sure he was with Gloria.

The next day went by more quickly, and Sam hummed as she got ready for dinner. She was looking forward to seeing Trudy.

Sam had decided to dress casually, wearing white slacks and an old favorite silk blouse splashed with flowers of blue and green. She stopped humming when she heard Derek's tap on her door. "Come in," she called.

He grinned at her. "Trudy's here, songbird." He was dressed in the same fashion she was, wearing trousers of white twill and a shirt of blue silk, the same shade as his eyes. For a moment it was as if she were seeing him for the first time again, and she caught her breath. How can anyone be so handsome? she thought.

Mrs. Holmes had fixed a marvelous dinner for them, but it was the camaraderie Sam would always remember. Trudy told her stories of Derek's boyhood, making Sam feel she had been there. There was a good deal of laughter, one remembrance leading to another, and Sam thought she had never seen Derek so relaxed. They were having coffee when Mrs. Holmes came into the room and told Derek there was a phone call for him.

Trudy and Sam took their coffee out to the porch and sat together on the sofa. Trudy said quietly, "Mrs. Holmes can't hear us out here, and Phillip's gone into town. So how are things going?"

Sam sighed. "It's not easy, Trudy—all this pretending. But Derek tries to make things go as smoothly as possible, and I don't think we've made any bad slips yet."

Trudy's eyes seemed to probe Sam's. "I didn't think it would be easy for you, Sam. Or for Derek, either."

Sam shook her head. "No. I think lying to Judge Norton and his wife bothered Derek terribly, but . . . I guess it's necessary."

Trudy sipped her coffee. "Has Derek told you why he's doing this?" As Sam shook her head, the older woman's eyes seemed to grow even sharper. "No? You seem so . . . I don't know . . . in tune with one another, I thought maybe . . ."

Sam looked into her cup. "I know. That's a strange thing. I feel as if I know him so well." She laughed in sudden embarrassment. "I guess being married, even this kind of marriage, makes you know someone . . ."

Trudy laughed, and reached out to pat Sam's hand. "That, or maybe you and Derek are just . . . what is that wonderful word? Yes, *simpático*. Could be, hmm?"

Sam reddened as Trudy watched her, eyes sparkling. "Ah, I thought so," Trudy said. "If you want him, child, why don't you go after him?"

"Trudy!" Sam protested. "I don't—"

The older woman waved Sam's objections aside with a toss of her hand. "Come on, Sam. That's what G.G. would do, *is* doing, as a matter of fact, even though she thinks he's a happily married bridegroom."

What do I care? Sam asked herself, but the words popped out anyhow. "Gloria's . . . going after him?"

Trudy snorted. "It's disgusting. She's hanging on him every minute. There are a lot of reports due the end of the month, and she's already talking about how much easier it would be to work nights at her apartment, getting them out."

Sam looked through the screen at the ocean in the distance. "Well, Trudy, you know as well as I do—that really is none of my business."

"Hmph." The sharp eyes dismissed Sam's words. "Did they—Derek and Gloria—ever go out together?"

"They did. Only because she made such a nuisance of herself, and Derek didn't care. Or maybe he thought she needed a friend. She's in the process of a messy divorce, and she's spent a lot of time crying on Derek's shoulder about her stingy husband—you know the type of thing. All she wants is eighty percent of everything he owns, which is plenty."

Sam nodded, and Trudy went on, "Anyhow, that's why Derek took her out. He sees that she's a lot like Vicky, so he figures he's immune. But it worries me, because she's a lot trickier than he is, and the worst thing that could happen to him would be to get tangled up with someone like that again."

"Yes," Sam said. "Well, I hope that doesn't happen. Derek deserves better than that."

Trudy's voice was persuasive. "On the other hand, someone like *you* . . ."

"Oh, Trudy," Sam said miserably, "you don't know . . ." Her voice trailed off as Trudy watched her, waiting for her to say more. She was relieved when Derek joined them, saving her from blurting out her thought—Someone like me is the last thing any man needs!

Trudy left soon afterward, Sam and Derek walking out to the courtyard where her car was parked. Derek embraced his aunt and said, "Well, Trudy, what do you think? Will Sam and I be able to fool the sharpest eyes in Spencer Industries?"

"I don't think you'll have any problem at all. Just act natural," she said innocently, and drove away.

Derek turned to look at Sam, eyes narrowed. Then he laughed shortly and said, "That Trudy. How about a walk on the beach, Sam?"

They left their shoes on the terrace and rolled up pants legs against capricious waves, then walked down to the sand. The moon was full, the beach glimmering silver. Sam sighed, and thought, if only things were always this simple, if she could just walk along this beach forever. With Derek . . . her mind turned away from the thought.

He had stopped, facing her. "Sam," he said, studying her face, her lips. For a moment she looked at him, wanting nothing more than to fly into his arms. Then she turned away. "No, Derek," she whispered, beginning to walk back toward the villa.

He followed her, silent for a few moments. Then

he said casually, "It was a pleasant evening, wasn't it?"

"Yes," Sam said, grateful for a safe topic. "I enjoyed talking with Trudy."

"And me?" he asked, smiling. "We get along well, don't we, Sam? At least—" His smile faded. "At least as long as I don't touch you."

"Don't, Derek!" Sam said, the words torn from her at the pain in his voice. "It's not you—it's my problem. Please . . ."

But he had walked on ahead, not hearing.

Derek told her most people just wore bathing suits to the company picnic, but Sam had shuddered at the thought of wearing her pink bikini. She had decided on her favorite swimsuit. Rather modest by Colette's standards, it was a one-piece suit of yellow flowers on a white background. Over it she slipped a yellow terrycloth beach jacket with a drawstring waist. In the Mercedes on the way to the picnic Derek chuckled at her constant fiddling with the bow.

"Relax, Sam. You look great. We won't stay too long, just put in an appearance."

"I know," she said, "but I want to look right. After all," she added mischievously, "you don't want one of your employees to see me and say, 'He married *her*?', do you?"

Derek laughed heartily. "Fat chance. And you know it," he said, arching a brow in mockery. "But just remember, you absolutely *adore* me."

"I'll force myself," she said dryly.

They had waited until late afternoon to go, and the party was in full swing. A volleyball game was in progress, and hamburgers and hot dogs sizzled on a charcoal grill. From a cottage came the sound of dance music. Everyone seemed to be having a good time.

They accepted beer in paper cups, then walked around, Derek introducing Sam to various employees. A tall, thin man with faded red hair proved to be Vicky's uncle. Sam wondered if Derek had hired him because of the relationship.

They walked up the steps to the cottage, where the wooden floor shook from the energetic dancing within. As soon as they were inside, blinking in the dimness after the bright sunlight, Sam heard Gloria's throaty voice. "Well, look who finally showed up! Hi, Derek, Mrs. Spencer."

"Please, call me Sam."

Gloria's green eyes widened in exaggerated surprise. "Sam? Well, if you insist . . ."

"It's short for Samantha, Gloria," Derek said.

"Oh. Well, I just thought Sam was a boy's name, but I guess it's kinda cute," she said, her cool green eyes appraising Sam.

I *look* like a boy next to her, Sam thought. Gloria wore—almost—the tiniest of green bikinis on her startlingly white skin. A large square of green material draped carelessly around her waist, tied at one hip, served to make her look more nearly nude, rather than less. Her beauty, the flaming red hair and emerald green eyes, made her seem even more flamboyant than she had the first day Sam had met her.

"So how is married life?" Gloria asked. Her tone made Sam start guiltily, as if she knew the marriage was a farce.

"It's fine," Derek answered, putting an arm around Sam's shoulders. "Isn't it, darling?"

"Yes, of course," Sam said, forcing a smile. Seeing those shrewd green eyes on her, she snuggled into

Derek's embrace. "Just wonderful," she said sweetly, looking up at him.

"Well," Gloria said. "Let me introduce you to my date. Jeff!" she called across the room. "Jeff! Over here, honey."

Jeff Templeton was a tall, sandy-haired man with brown eyes. He and Gloria seemed very casual together. That's because Gloria isn't interested in him, Sam realized. She's after Derek.

As if to confirm Sam's suspicions, Gloria said, "What about it, boss? Can your new wife spare you for a few minutes, to dance with your old secretary?"

Derek glanced at Sam, who smiled and nodded. Inwardly she said, Trudy, girl, you were right about Gloria. But it's none of my business.

"Why don't we try it, Sam?" Jeff was saying.

"All right," she said, and they moved onto the dance floor. He was a good dancer, even for someone as nervous as Sam. He didn't hold her too close, and she relaxed, enjoying the romantic ballad.

"So you two just got married?" he asked.

"Yes, last week." To change the subject she said, "Have you and Gloria been going together long?"

"No, not at all. As a matter of fact, I haven't seen Gloria since we were in high school together. I just got into town yesterday and called her then, and she invited me to the picnic."

He switched the conversation onto more general topics, and Sam thought perhaps he didn't want to answer questions either. From the corner of her eye she saw Gloria wheedle Derek into one more dance, and she and Jeff sat it out. Talking with him seemed to flow as smoothly as the dancing, but at the end of it all she knew about him was that he was an attorney with a practice somewhere in Georgia, and he had a flattering manner of hanging onto every word she said.

This aspect of his personality puzzled Sam, but she decided being a good listener was probably a trait he had developed carefully, as an asset for a young attorney. He *was* remarkably easy to talk to.

"You really must be henpecking this poor man, Sam," Gloria said as she and Derek returned. "He insisted he couldn't stay for another dance."

Sam linked her arm with Derek's. "Oh, he could have—if he'd wanted to," she said sweetly.

Derek's mouth twitched. "You know how newlyweds are. We just don't like being separated for very long, Gloria."

Gloria opened her mouth to reply, but Jeff said, "Come on, Glory. That sounds like one of our old songs," and they left.

Derek's tone was solicitous. "Would you like anything, darling? Another beer? A saucer of milk, maybe?"

She looked up to see the laughter in his eyes, and had to giggle. "No, thanks. Maybe I'll just wait and have a bite of catfood with Tiptoe when we get home."

"In the meantime, how about a swim?"

They waded into the ocean together, holding hands for the benefit of any onlookers. Glancing around, Derek said, "You handled that beautifully, by the way."

"What do you mean—Gloria?"

He nodded. "A new bride, another woman monopolizing her husband—yes, I think she might make a remark on the catty side. Very true-to-life." Why was he watching her so closely?

They were deep enough to swim now, the waves lifting Sam off her feet when they swelled in.

"Very . . . adoring wife, just as I asked. You're a

105

good actress," Derek went on. Now the mocking light was back in his remarkable blue eyes. "Or were you acting?"

"Oh!" She turned toward him, angry, and saw his mouth curling, the laughter beginning. She shoved a handful of ocean at him. "You!"

He laughed and reached for her. "For that I'm going to duck you!"

"First you have to catch me!" she yelled, swimming away from him. She was a good swimmer, and she was sure she could get away from him, sure he was too big to be anything but clumsy in the water.

He surprised her, pulling her under by her ankles. She came up sputtering, and swam toward him. "Now it's your turn, Derek!" she called. But he stood his ground. When she reached him and put her hands on his shoulders, she couldn't budge him.

"Oh, now that's not fair," she said, and then his eyes caught hers. A wave pushed her against him, and she was in his arms. "Derek . . ." she murmured, as he brought his lips to hers. For a moment she clung to him, drawn to his warmth in the midst of the swirling coolness around them. Then she knew, with a kind of despair, that if she let this continue, she would once more face the nightmares Kyle had left her, the fear.

"No, Derek," she moaned, trying to push him away.

"Sam," he said huskily. "It's me, not—don't turn away from me." He tried to draw her back into his arms, but she fought him with rising panic.

Seeing her fear he released her. "All right, Sam, all right. Don't be afraid."

He grasped her arm to steady her against the waves, and she looked away, grateful for his strength, ashamed of her fears. How foolishly immature she must seem to him!

They began to walk in toward shore. She looked up at him. "Derek, I'm—"

"Never mind, Sam," he said gently. "Get ready to smile, though. We've got an audience waiting."

Sam looked at the beach to see Jeff Templeton waving at them. "Hi—we're just going to get something to eat. Want to join us?" he called.

"Damn," Derek muttered under his breath. "I guess we can't get out of it." He nodded and waved to Jeff, then turned to Sam as they reached shore and whispered, "That swim *did* make me hungry. How about you?"

"Yes, I'm starving—" Sam began, then looked at him to see his eyes dancing with delight and realized his meaning. "You're impossible." She grinned, shaking her head.

They retrieved their beach wraps from the sand and joined Gloria and Jeff. Sam noticed Gloria watching them through narrowed eyes and was suddenly sure she had witnessed the kiss, and her fear-ridden rejection.

The four of them filled paper plates with hot dogs and potato salad, and carried them to a picnic table. On the surface, conversation seemed to flow easily, but Sam had the feeling Gloria was weighing every word she and Derek said, judging their performance in the part of newlyweds. That's ridiculous, she told herself. She can't possibly know the truth.

"Sam," Jeff was saying, laughing. "Wake up."

"What? Oh, I'm sorry. I guess I was thinking— what did you say?"

Jeff smiled at her, his voice friendly. "I said I love your drawl. It doesn't sound like a Florida accent, though."

"Oh," she said, laughing. "No. Try the hills of Tennessee."

There was silence for a moment, then Gloria said, "I thought you were from Atlanta, Sam."

Sam looked at Derek. "Well, I—"

"Sam's lived in Atlanta the past few years, Gloria, but she grew up in Tennessee," Derek said smoothly, rising. "Would anyone like another hot dog?"

"I would," Gloria said. "I'll go with you, Derek. That is, if your wife doesn't mind," she added in saccharine tones.

"Be my guest," Sam said dryly, half-irritated at the way the redhead clung to Derek's arm, half-relieved to be free of the questions in her eyes.

She looked up to find Jeff watching her, and blushed, knowing how accurately her face mirrored her thoughts.

"Gloria can be a little pushy, can't she?" he said. "I guess she was sort of disappointed when Derek got married. I understand they dated some, but . . . well, surely you know *you* don't need to worry about someone like Gloria!"

"Jeff—" Sam began, embarrassed.

"No, really," he said earnestly, "I guess I shouldn't be saying this, but you're worth ten Glorias, and I'm sure Derek realizes it." He stopped, laughing shortly. "I'm sorry, Sam. I don't mean to embarrass you. I just hate to see you letting her upset you. Gloria's okay, as long as you don't take her too seriously."

Sam smiled, feeling awkward after Jeff's outburst, but grateful as well. It was nice to have an ally.

Gloria and Derek returned. Sam wondered sourly how she managed to balance a paper plate in the wind and hang onto Derek's arm so securely at the same time.

Sam breathed a sigh of relief when at last they had eaten and said their good-byes. The Mercedes seemed a haven where she could give up pretence for a while.

Derek chuckled as she leaned her head back and closed her eyes. "That bad, was it?" he said.

She turned her head lazily to smile at him. "Not really, except the last part. How about you? Did Gloria have a lot of questions about what part of Tennessee I was from, and when I moved to Atlanta, and why on earth you married me anyhow?"

He laughed. "Nothing I couldn't handle. Gloria's easily diverted."

"I'll bet."

He grinned at her. "What is this, Mrs. Spencer? Jealous wife time?"

"Of course not," Sam said. "But if I *were* your wife—I mean if we—you know what I mean. If we were *really* married, I would find it very hard to put up with Gloria."

He laughed again, but there was an edge in his voice as he said, "And if we were *really* married, I'd be tempted to punch your friend Jeff."

"Jeff! Why?" Sam asked, sitting up in surprise.

"Come on, Sam," he said impatiently. "The man was . . . fawning over you. Talking about your delightful accent, asking a million questions—"

She reddened, remembering Jeff's outburst while Derek and Gloria were gone. "Oh, Derek—he's just very young, that's all."

"Young? Sam, the man is thirty—that's five years older than you, my child!"

"Well, he seems younger," she said stubbornly.

"Just don't forget, you are *supposed* to be a new bride, and not particularly receptive to any . . . overtures from other men, no matter how young they are!"

She looked at him openmouthed, not believing for a moment that he was serious, but his face was grave, his eyes on the road. "You might remember that piece of advice yourself," she replied coolly.

Seven

That coolness seemed to stay with them for the weekend. Derek hardly spoke to Sam until Monday morning when he told her he had taken the day off to pick up Debby at the airport and spend some time with her.

"We'll be home for lunch," he told Sam. "Make an effort to get along with her, will you? It's important."

"Of course I will," she answered, but as he drove away she wondered why that was important. She wouldn't be here very long anyhow.

The morning dragged by, with Sam becoming ever more nervous at the prospect of meeting Debby. You're being silly, Sam, she told herself sternly as she combed her hair and checked her makeup for the fourth time, but when she heard the car in the drive she jumped.

She met them at the front door. Debby didn't seem nearly so formidable in person as in Sam's imagination. She was a pretty nine-year-old with long black curls and her father's blue eyes.

Sam extended a hand. "Hi, Debby. I'm Sam."

The child ignored the hand, looking over Sam's shoulder into the living room. "Hi," she said noncommitally. "Where's the cat?"

"Why, I don't know. Probably on the sunporch," Sam answered. "Would you like—" But the child was gone, running through the living room door.

Sam stood up. Derek shrugged. "I'm sorry, Sam. She's upset about leaving her grandparents. The only thing I could get her to show any interest in was Tiptoe. Give her time."

Sam walked inside with him and down the hallway. At the door to his room he said, "Would you come in here for a moment? I want to talk with you."

When they were inside he said, "I know she's probably going to come across as a spoiled brat, Sam, but she's not really. Or she wasn't, anyhow. But Vicky's parents . . ." He ran a hand tiredly through his crisply curling hair.

"It's all right, Derek. And I doubt if she's a spoiled brat. As you say, she's upset about leaving her grandparents. How long has she been staying with them?"

He scowled. "That's part of the problem. When Vicky and I separated, she took Debby. Not because she wanted her, but because *I* did. Oh, hell, I guess I'm sounding bitter, aren't I?"

Sam winced at the pain in his voice, touching his hand. He took a deep breath. "Anyhow, when Vicky died, her parents convinced me it would be better for Debby to stay there for a while. They said it would be too much for her, losing her mother and then being taken away from the home she was used to. . . . I don't know, it made sense at the time. I thought it would be selfish of me to insist, but now . . ."

"It'll be all right, Derek," Sam said, reassuring him.

During lunch she began to believe it *would* be all right, at least as far as Derek was concerned. Debby asked him several questions about the house and the beach. She pointedly ignored Sam, however, determined not to like her new stepmother.

Well, that doesn't matter, Sam thought, as long as she gives Derek a chance. Watching his face as he talked to his daughter, his pride and love obvious, she was touched.

After lunch Debby retreated to her bedroom with a stack of comic books. Derek looked after her with some exasperation, but Sam smiled, remembering her own feelings at that age. "She'll be out later, Derek, with a million things to talk to you about. Don't worry."

The phone rang and Derek answered it. From his end of the conversation, Sam could tell that it was Gloria. When he hung up, he said, "I've got to go in to the office, Sam. It's an emergency, and it may take quite a while to clear up."

Sam bit back a remark about Gloria and her so-called emergencies, saying simply, "All right," and walking down the hall to her room. She was like Debby, she thought wryly, going into her own retreat.

She took a nap, and when she woke and looked out the window, the horizon was purple with thunderclouds. She tapped on Derek's door, but he wasn't home yet.

Sam sighed. She didn't like long afternoons, particularly when they included lightning. She wandered onto the sunporch to watch the storm, with a kind of bravado. Tiptoe was asleep on the wicker chair, but when she sat down on the sofa, he seemed to bound from the chair to her lap without opening his eyes, and went back to sleep.

They had had storms like this in Tennessee, she remembered as the rain began pelting the sides of the house. She wondered what her father was doing, and how many lies she would have to tell him before this charade was over. She didn't realize she was crying until a teardrop fell on Tiptoe's fur as she stroked him.

"Sam?" Debby stood in the doorway, regarding her with nine-year-old solemnity. "What's wrong?"

Sam wiped her eyes hastily, thinking of more lies, the lies adults tell children, and decided this time there was nothing wrong with the truth. "I'm just a little homesick for my father."

"Oh," Debby said, sitting beside her, reaching out to pet the cat, who sighed and stretched. "Aren't you homesick for your mother too?"

"My mother passed away when I was a child, Debby."

"Oh. Like me," Debby said. "Did you live with your grandma and grandpa?" she asked, her young-old eyes watching Sam carefully.

"No. I was lucky enough—like you—to have a wonderful father to take care of me."

Debby nodded, stroking Tiptoe silently for a moment. Then she said, "Did your father marry someone else after your mother died?"

"No," Sam said softly, aching for the child's hurt.

"What if he had?" Debby asked, looking at Sam with a curious expression.

Sam considered the question. "Well, I guess it would depend on whether or not I liked her. If I didn't like her, I suppose I would have been pretty unhappy."

"Well, what if you did like her?"

"Then I guess we would have been friends."

Debby nodded and turned her attention back to the cat. "I wish he would sit on *my* lap," she said.

Sam grinned. "Let me show you something." She stood up, sliding Tiptoe onto the sofa cushion. The cat looked around for a moment, blinking, then spotted Debby. He stood and stretched, arching his back, and resettled himself on her lap.

Debby laughed delightedly. "He much prefers a warm lap to a chair for his naps," Sam said.

"Thank you, Sam," Debby said, smiling. This time her eyes looked like those of a little girl, and Sam longed to hug her.

Mrs. Holmes made a simple dinner of homemade soup and hot rolls. Sam and Debby ate alone, Derek still not having returned. The little girl chattered happily enough during the meal, and Sam was grateful for her company.

When Debby was ready for bed, Sam tucked her in. She was somewhat surprised that Debby didn't object to this motherly gesture, but it seemed her acceptance of Sam was as complete as it had been sudden. This time she did hug the child, and tears came to her eyes when Debby hugged back, saying, "I like you, Sam," in a shy whisper.

"I like you, too, Debby," she whispered back, and both grinned. When she closed Debby's door and went into her own room, though, Sam wondered if this were someone else who was going to be hurt by the lies she and Derek were telling. How let down was Debby going to be when—Never mind, she'd be living in town. We can still be friends, Sam told herself, pushing the thought away.

It was still early, but she decided to take a bath and go to bed. She soaked for a while, enjoying the luxury of the huge tub, easily twice as large as the one in her tiny apartment. Wrapped in a towel, she made a sound of annoyance as she remembered that her favorite nightgown—the football jersey—was in the hamper. She touched the frilly lingerie from Colette's shop and grimaced. Lacy nightgowns stirred too many unhappy memories of her marriage to Kyle.

Rummaging through the bureau, she found an old silk shirt her father had bought by mistake. It was much too big for him, and that much larger on Sam, but she liked it for sleeping. She put it on, not wanting to think about how much safer she felt when she hid her femininity. Would she never lose the scars of her marriage?

She got into bed and tried to read, but the book was not exciting enough to hold her interest, and not dull enough to put her to sleep. At last she tossed it aside with an exclamation of disgust. She walked over to the door and looked out at the ocean, then slid the door open and went out onto the terrace. She breathed deeply, loving the breeze off the Atlantic, the fresh smell of the earth after a storm.

A chuckle behind her made her jump. "Sam, where on earth do you get those fetching sleeping garments of yours?" Derek said from the chaise longue.

"Oh—I didn't know you were home," she said, tugging at the shirt. She hoped all the buttons were done.

"I haven't been here long," he said. "How did it go with Debby?"

Sam pulled a chair close to his. "I think it went pretty well."

He took a deep breath. "I hope so. She seemed to be opening up to me a little at lunch, but she was . . . well, almost hostile to you. I hate to see that."

Sam nodded. "Yes, but we made some progress

this afternoon," she said, and told him of the day's events.

He was delighted. "That's wonderful, Sam. I'm relieved."

"Yes, but—Derek, what about when we . . . we get a divorce? We should plan ahead, handle it so that Debby isn't hurt. . . . Maybe it would be better if she *didn't* like me," Sam said ruefully.

His face softened. "Knowing you, I should have realized you'd be worried about that. Look—" He hesitated a moment, then said, "Let's just cross that bridge when we come to it. In the meantime, I'd like for you two to be friends. Even after—afterwards, when we're . . ." He stopped for a moment. "I guess I have no right to ask you to be concerned about her after we're divorced. I'm sure you'll be too busy getting your own life back in order."

Something in his voice made Sam's eyes fill with tears. She stood and walked over to the low wall that surrounded the terrace. "Don't be silly, Derek. I won't be too busy. I'd like to keep in touch with her."

He crossed the terrace to stand beside her. She looked up at him with anger in her eyes. "Do you really think I could . . . could befriend her, win her trust—under false pretences, I might add—and then just abandon her? The poor child has lost her mother already—I'm not about to add to her sense of loss by—"

She stopped when he laid a hand gently on her lips, smiling. "All right, I apologize," he said. "I should have known better. I certainly should have known," he said softly.

A sudden gust from the ocean made Sam shiver. "Are you cold?" Derek asked. Before she could answer, he was unbuttoning his shirt of apricot silk.

"Derek, what—?"

Grinning down at her, he slipped the shirt over her shoulders. "Another garment for your collection, Sam," he teased. With a gentle hand under her chin, he tilted her face up, searching her eyes. "Tell me, does each one represent a heart you've won?"

"Of course not. I—" She stopped, wondering if he'd meant— Then his face blotted out the moon and his lips covered hers. He made no move to take her in his arms, but only stood there, his hand warm against her face, while his mouth explored hers with gentle insistence. It would have been easy to push him away, except for the blood pounding in her ears, drowning out even the sound of the ocean. Her legs suddenly felt boneless, incapable of supporting her weight.

When he released her for a moment, she could almost think again. What was it he said? But before she could capture the elusive thought, his arms went around her, pulling her body to his. She could feel the heat of his bare chest, the roughness of the hair on it, through the silk shirt she wore. He moaned, "Sam . . ." as his mouth moved from her lips to her throat. His hands caressed her back, pulling her yet closer to him. She felt his shirt fall from her shoulders as she lifted her arms, returning his embrace.

His hands moved to her hips, drawing her to him. She gasped at his closeness, knowing his need matched hers. Her need, that she had not acknowledged, because she had never felt this longing so keenly before, the aching desire to belong to this man, and to possess him as well. Now she knew what it was to want someone, Sam thought dazedly, winding her fingers in Derek's hair, kissing his face urgently. She had never felt this way with Kyle— don't think about it now, mustn't think about Kyle, she told herself as a dart of fear touched the corner of her mind.

His hands fumbled with the buttons of her shirt, opening it, touching her breasts. He bent to take a taut nipple into his mouth, and Sam moaned, cradling his head in her hands. He stood and looked into her eyes, then let his gaze travel over her body, naked now except for the open shirt and brief bikini panties. She was glad for the moonlight, the desire she read on his face feeding the flame that was rising inside her.

"Sam, let me show you the way it can be, should be," he said huskily. He picked her up effortlessly, and she felt herself being carried across the terrace, mindful of nothing but his lips on hers, his tongue probing her mouth.

He shifted her weight in his arms to open the sliding door, and she remembered another time, another door. Kyle had carried her into their bedroom, only then she had been screaming, begging him to let her go—

"No, Derek . . ." she protested, the words mumbled as she tried to escape his lips.

"Yes," he said firmly, capturing her mouth once more as he closed the door. He laid her on the bed she had left such a short time before, trailing a gentle hand down her body, making her gasp with pleasure.

Derek lay down beside her, rolling partly on top of her, and suddenly she felt trapped. She remembered with sickening clarity being carried into a bedroom and trapped in that fashion, and Kyle's face swam cruelly before her.

"No!" she cried, struggling to free herself.

Derek held her flailing arms. "Sam," he said softly. "It's all right. It's me, Derek. I won't hurt you—trust me, little one . . ." He tried to kiss her, but she turned her face from side to side wildly, in a frenzy of fear.

Part of Sam's mind told her not to be afraid, that this was Derek, gentle Derek—but another part could only remember a brutal man who had also promised not to hurt her.

"Then let me go!" she cried. Seeking words to hurt him, to make him release her, she said, "Maybe I should have made *you* sign a contract!"

He rolled away from her immediately and stood. When she dared to look up at him, she saw that his eyes blazed in a white face. She clambered off the bed and buttoned her shirt with trembling fingers, turning her back to him.

He gripped her shoulders and spun her around with a force that frightened her. He held her, thrusting his face close to hers and said, in a voice full of fury, "Now listen to me—I'm well aware that we had a business agreement. I know that you wanted it to be just that—strictly business, and I told you it would be. But I didn't count on falling in love with you. The last thing I needed was a funny little bird with a broken wing—parading around in outsized shirts, thinking they hide her beauty, when all the time they only make her irresistible—" His voice softened, and he said, "If you really wanted us to be just business partners, why did you have to be so dear, and so vulnerable?"

Sam was stunned by his words. "Derek, I . . . I didn't mean . . . to lead you on." She slumped onto the bed and ran her fingers through her hair in a gesture of hopelessness. "I was . . . am . . . attracted to you, but there's no point . . ."

He watched her, listening to her carefully. He knelt

in front of her, his eyes level with hers. "What are you trying to say, Sam?" he asked gently.

She swallowed painfully. "I . . . I can't . . . get involved with anyone, Derek. I don't intend ever to marry—I mean not a real marriage." She put her hands over her face, covering the tears. "I'm frigid," she whispered.

"What!" He stood and walked to the window. She turned to look at him and saw his shoulders shaking a second before the boom of his laughter rang out. "Oh, Sam!" he gasped. "You are many things— the words frustrating, irritating, and impossible come to mind—but not frigid, never that!"

She stared at him with stony eyes. He returned to kneel before her once again, his eyes seeming to search her mind. "Ah, Sam, don't you know you're the warmest, most loving woman I've ever met?" His hand touched her cheek with infinite tenderness. "And I love you with all my heart. I want to know what your feelings are for me."

For a moment she looked at his face, the blue eyes warm, with no trace of mockery in them now, the firm, gentle mouth, unaware of the expression of yearning he could read clearly in her own eyes.

"I told you, Derek," she said softly. "I'm attracted to you. You're a very handsome man, you know," she added, smiling. "But . . . it's no use."

"I think maybe it's a little more than that, Sam," he said, his eyes caressing her face. "And someday you'll know that too. But for now, I'm giving you notice," he said, his voice tender, "that I'm changing the terms of the contract. I want this to be a real marriage."

"But you promised—" Sam began, drawing back in anger, and the beginning of fear.

"I told you, I didn't count on falling in love with

121

you. But don't worry, Sam. I can wait until you're ready to go along with what your own instincts tell you is right. I'm a patient man." He leaned forward and kissed her lips gently, then with obvious reluctance walked toward his own bedroom. In the doorway, he turned. "Maybe you'd better go back to your old habit of keeping the door locked—I'm not all *that* patient."

Eight

After he left Sam sat numbly, looking at the closed door. He loves me—Derek loves me! For a moment she longed to hug herself girlishly, to dance about the room believing in fairy tales, to believe that Cinderella and her Prince Charming lived happily ever after—but then the rumpled bed caught her eye.

That's what marriage is, she thought. How can I possibly be Derek's wife? Weren't the years with Kyle enough to show me—and yet . . . She remembered Derek's kisses, his hands caressing her, with a vividness that made a warm flush spread over her body.

She walked over to the door slowly, hesitating. For a moment she had the impulse to push it open and fling herself into Derek's bed, but instead she turned the lock. From the next room she heard a low chuckle. "Very wise, Sam. Don't forget the terrace door," he said, and she could picture him, lying in his bed, smiling.

She left the terrace door open so she could hear the ocean, and fell asleep smiling.

Sam felt strangely shy when she went into the dining room the next morning, and was disappointed to find that Derek had already left.

Mrs. Holmes said, "Oh, yes, that husband of yours is a hard worker. He said that since he took yesterday morning off he needed to go in early today. Let me fix you some eggs, Mrs. Spencer."

"No, thank you," Sam said. "I'm not hungry this morning."

Mrs. Holmes rolled her eyes skyward and sighed, "Love!" and Sam blushed.

She walked out to the terrace and saw a patch of apricot silk caught on one of the lounge chairs. Derek's shirt. She picked it up and held it to her face, inhaling his scent, remembering how he had slipped it on her shoulders the night before. The silk felt cool on her cheek, comforting to her touch. Everything about Derek made her feel safe—except his passion.

She lay back on the chaise longue holding the shirt. She wondered if he would settle for a marriage with every kind of love except physical, she thought. Then her mouth curled at the thought of what he would say—or do—at the suggestion of such a thing.

She laughed under her breath. No, she couldn't imagine Derek agreeing to that. She could almost hear him saying, "I don't need a *buddy*, Sam."

And you, Sam? Would *you* be willing to settle for a marriage like that? Once she would have answered yes, but all the new feelings Derek had aroused in her made her wonder. Maybe, in time . . .

She decided to walk on the beach, and went into

her bedroom to leave her shoes. She hung Derek's shirt in the closet.

The ocean worked its usual magic for Sam, making her problems seem far away, the permanence of its rumbling soothing her. She thought for the millionth time that if world leaders had to take their shoes off and sit with their feet in the ocean to discuss affairs of state, there would be no more wars. She smiled at the whimsical thought, and at the seagulls, and at life.

When Sam walked back onto the terrace, her cheeks were glowing, her eyes alight, and when Derek appeared from his room, her heart leapt with a joy that was clearly visible to him. "Derek! What are you doing home so soon?"

"If I had known it was going to make you this happy, I'd have been here sooner," he said, smiling. "Sam, you're so beautiful—"

Sam suddenly felt awkward, shy as a teenager. "It's just . . . I wasn't expecting you. Did you take the day off?" she asked.

He shook his head. "I came home to pack. I have to go to Atlanta for a few days." He sat on the low terrace wall.

Sam's face fell. "Oh," she said, disappointed. Then she saw his watchful eyes, measuring her reaction. "Well, I guess business is business, right?" she said with forced cheerfulness, sitting down beside him.

"Come with me, Sam," he said.

She looked at him. "To Atlanta?"

He nodded. "I'll be there the rest of the week. I have a room at the hotel where we stayed before."

A room. One room. Had he emphasized the singular noun, or had she imagined it? No, she saw his mouth twitch as she considered it. His eyes caught hers, urging her to say yes.

Sam cleared her throat. "No, I . . . I guess I should stay here. Debby . . ."

He shook his head, grinning. "The truth, Sam. We're both sick of lies anyway—there's no need for us to lie to each other."

She looked down at her feet. "I'm not ready, Derek."

His arm went around her shoulders, hugging her. She was surprised to hear him laugh softly. "That's better anyhow. We've progressed from 'Never' to 'Not yet.'"

Feeling she was losing ground, confused, Sam said, "Now wait—I didn't mean . . . I didn't say that I would ever . . ."

Her voice trailed off as she saw the slow smile spread across his face, his eyes tracing the line of her lips. "Oh, you will, Sam. You will," he whispered. His eyes holding her, she sat motionless beside him, wanting him to kiss her. When he chuckled she realized that, once again, he had known what was going on in her mind. Cheeks flaming, she stood quickly.

"Hadn't you better finish packing?" she asked coolly. When he walked into his bedroom he was still chuckling.

When Sam watched him drive off, she was tempted to run after him, shouting that she'd changed her mind. That would *really* make him laugh, she thought sourly. No, it's just as well that I have a few days to think things over. Besides, he'll be back Friday night.

She walked into the sunporch and sat down. I'm going to miss him, she realized. She tried to imagine what her life would be like in six months, if they . . . no, *when* they separated. Her little world that had been so satisfactory—her apartment, Tiptoe, a job, even the ocean—now seemed not enough some-how.

Debby came into the room, looking for Tiptoe. He was apparently outside exploring his new territory, and Sam suggested she and Debby go shell-hunting. They packed a picnic lunch, and the rest of the day passed most agreeably. They returned home at sundown, tired and happy.

. After Debby was in bed, Sam went in to give her a final goodnight hug. Sam felt tears in her throat when Debby said, "You know what, Sam? I like it here. I love you and Daddy so much."

Sam hugged her again. "I love you, too, Deb."

The child giggled at the new nickname, and said, "And you love Daddy too, don't you?"

Sam brushed a curl back from the smooth young forehead. She said gravely, "Yes, I do. Now, time to sleep, okay?"

In her own room Sam walked across to stare out at the moonlit sky. She hadn't lied to Debby, she thought. She loved him. She hadn't wanted to, but she did.

The next afternoon Sam was reading on the ter-race when she heard a car in the drive. A few min-utes later Mrs. Holmes brought Jeff Templeton out.

"I hope you don't mind, Sam. I was in the neigh-borhood—"

Mrs. Holmes asked if they would like some iced tea, and Sam looked at Jeff inquiringly. "Yes, please," he said. "It's hot out today."

Sam was surprised to see him. When they had left the company picnic, she and Derek had made the usual polite invitations, but she hadn't expected Jeff to drop by, particularly in the afternoon when Derek was out.

You're being old-fashioned, Sam, a voice inside her chided. There's no reason you shouldn't have company when Derek's gone.

Mrs. Holmes brought the tea. When she had left, Jeff said again, "I hope you don't mind my dropping by. I thought, with Derek out of town, you could use someone to talk to."

His face was so open and boyish that Sam was ashamed of her misgivings. He was right, she *could* use someone to talk to.

She wondered how he knew Derek was out of town, but then he began to tell her a story about one of his first cases as an attorney, and she forgot to ask. They had a pleasant afternoon on the terrace, except for one uncomfortable moment when Sam sensed something in the way Jeff said her name— she was suddenly reminded of a summer at home, between her first and second years of college, when the teen-aged boy who lived next door to her developed a crush on her. It was flattering, but a strain as well. No matter what Derek said about Jeff's age, he seemed very young to her.

The next day was Thursday, and Sam found herself counting the hours until Derek would be back on Friday evening. She invited Trudy to dinner Thursday night, thinking that would be a much more prudent way to fill her need for company than talking to Jeff Templeton.

Debby talked a blue streak all through dinner. She adored her great-aunt Trudy, and it was obvious that the feeling was mutual. She had Trudy gasping with laughter at her accounts of Tiptoe's antics. Sam smiled happily, thinking how different Debby seemed from the cool, somewhat sullen child she had first thought her. She's so like Derek, she

thought. She has that same wonderful openness. . . .
Sam looked up to meet Trudy's understanding eyes.

Later Sam and Trudy had coffee on the sunporch.
Trudy put her feet up on a stool and sighed. "Well.
Things are looking good," she said in a satisfied
tone.

Sam grinned at her. "All right, Trudy. What are
you getting at?"

"You know very well, young lady. You think Debby's
terrific, and she thinks you're the greatest thing
since sliced bread. Derek adores you. And I have a
feeling *that's* a two-way street, too. You all belong
together. Simple," she said, shrugging expressively.

Sam had to laugh at the neat way Trudy tied
the whole package up. "It sounds simple, I admit,
but . . ."

"And it is," Trudy said firmly.

Sam sighed. "It's not that easy, Trudy," she said
miserably. "There are things you don't know. . . ."

"Am I right about the way Debby feels? I *know*
Derek loves you, I'd have to be blind to see the way
he looks at you and not know. . . . And you, Sam?
You *do* care for him, don't you?"

Sam nodded. "Yes, but—"

Trudy stood up. "Then the things I don't know
don't matter. Whatever they are, and I mean *whatever*. The important stuff is right, the rest can be
worked out."

Sam stood. "Are you leaving already?" she asked,
a token protest, since she was afraid of Trudy's
questions, her sharp eyes.

"Yes," she said, and laughed. "So you're off the
spot for now, missy. But you need to do some serious thinking. I'm going to take the day off tomorrow
and take my great-niece shopping. School starts in
a few weeks, so she can probably use some new

clothes. Now, I don't want any arguments from you,"
she said sternly. "Derek will be home tomorrow night,
and I want you to have all day to decide if you really
want to lose a catch like him."

Sam could only laugh in exasperation, and agree
to have Debby ready at nine.

She lay awake a long time after she turned out her
light. Trudy's right, she thought. Derek did love her,
and she loved him. Simple. Only . . . what about
the terrible memories? When Derek made love to her,
was she always going to see Kyle? To have the same
cold marriage with Derek as she'd had with him—no,
it was unthinkable. She couldn't bear to see Derek
turn against her like that, she loved him too much.

But she had so many feelings with him, for him,
that she had never known in her marriage to Kyle.
Maybe this time it would be different. . . .

Friday morning was steamy hot, with storm clouds
in the distance promising relief later in the day.
Sam decided to walk down to the cove and swim.
Trudy had left, taking Debby, with a final injunction:
"Think." Well, the cove would be a good place for
that, although her thoughts merely seemed to run
in circles, in any case.

She picked up the tiny bikini from Colette's shop,
hesitating. Why not? No one will see me at the cove,
she thought, and I certainly ought to improve my
tan with this bit of pink nothing.

For a while she sunbathed, enjoying the sun's
rays on her back. Then she sat up and looked at the
surf, remembering what Derek had said about listening to what the ocean had to say about his problems.
Well, Atlantic, she thought wryly, it's like this: I love
him and he loves me, and we should live happily
ever after—but would we? Do I dare take a chance?

I've finally gotten over the pain of my first marriage—well, no. Not really, that's the problem. But I've gotten to the point where I can live a reasonably happy, if lonely, life. Do I really want to make myself vulnerable to someone again?

And indeed, the ocean did give her its answer: Too late, too late, the surf seemed to whisper. "Yes," she whispered, "it's too late. I'm already vulnerable where Derek is concerned."

Sighing, she waded into the foaming water, its coolness refreshing. She swam a few strokes and was pleasantly surprised to find that the bikini went with her through the water, half-expecting to see it floating out to sea.

She lay on her back and floated, thinking how pleasant, how tranquil, to give oneself up to the tides, be carried along—as she longed to let her feelings for Derek carry her along. But could she?

She swam until she could touch bottom, then began to walk back to shore. Looking up at the beach, she stopped, heart pounding. Derek! He was wearing swimming trunks and as she watched, he dropped his shirt on the sand and waved to her, then plunged into the ocean, swimming toward her with long strokes.

When he reached her she was breathing as heavily as he. "I thought you wouldn't be home until tonight," she said, trying to seem only casually pleased.

"I was in a hurry." He grinned. "I heard about this beautiful brunette who was just dying for a chance to duck me, and since I owe her one . . ."

Sam snorted. "Oh, no. You don't play fair, you bully."

He held his arms out, his tone teasing, "Come on, Sam, you can duck me." He splashed water at her face.

"That does it," she said, and rushed toward him to push him under. He went under, but he took Sam with him, wrapping her tight in his arms. His lips claimed hers with an urgency greater than the need for oxygen. She forgot about breathing, aware only of their bodies pressed together, arching toward him with an instinct as old as the ocean itself.

In a moment they came to the surface, gasping for air. He picked her up and carried her out of the water, to the beach at the farthest corner of the cove, where boulders provided a natural shelter. He had spread a blanket on the sand there, and Sam thought, He planned this. But it didn't matter.

Nothing mattered but the warmth of his mouth on hers. His hand pushed the flimsy bikini top aside to caress her breasts, then to taste them, making her shiver. He looked up at her. "Are you cold?" he asked softly. "No," she answered, smiling, reaching up to pull him back to her.

"Sam. Oh, Sam," he moaned, his hands touching her breasts and stomach, seeming to scorch her with their warmth.

She buried her face against the damp mat of his chest, caressing his shoulders and back, warm in the sun. His fingers slipped inside the elastic of the bikini bottom, then hesitated. "Sam?" he said, his voice husky.

"Yes, Derek," she whispered. "Oh, yes . . ."

His touch was gentle, making her long for him, until she cried, "Oh, Derek, please . . . I want you."

His kisses covered her face, as he crooned, "Oh, Sam, my dear, my love. I love you so."

"Derek, I lo—"

"Derek! Sam! Yoo-hoo, where are you?" Gloria's voice called from down the beach.

Derek muttered against Sam's throat, "Damn."

Sam scrambled frantically from under him, adjusting her bathing suit. Derek looked at her and grinned wryly. "I don't suppose you'd agree to being very quiet here and hoping she doesn't find us?"

She studied his face a moment and said, "You know, I believe you would."

His gaze traveled from her flushed cheeks down the length of her body, bringing a flush of warmth to the pit of her stomach. "Try me," he said softly.

She laughed, embarrassed. "We can't do that, Derek."

He stood up and reached a hand down for her, chuckling. "It's nice to know the idea tempts you, anyhow."

She took his hand and he pulled her to her feet, and then against his chest. "It *does*, doesn't it? Tempt you, I mean."

She felt herself trembling against his arm, her legs wobbly beneath her. "Yes," she said faintly.

He took a deep breath, as of relief. "Later," he said. Then he called, "We're over here in the cove, Gloria!"

"Well, *here* you are!" the redhead said throatily. "Really, Sam, I think you've had too much sun—your face is absolutely flaming!"

"We were just about to go back," Derek said, picking up the blanket. "What's the problem?"

"Problem?" Gloria said blankly. "Oh. Mr. Hartford is at the office, and positively *insists* on seeing you. I told him you had just gotten back from Atlanta, but . . . well, you know how he is."

Derek scowled. "I guess I'm going to have to drive in for a while, Sam." The three of them walked toward the house together.

"I hope you won't be lonely, Sam," Gloria said. "Oh, I know! Why don't I stay for a while and we can visit! We haven't really had a chance to get to know one another, and I smelled Mrs. Holmes's wonderful soup when I came through the house earlier—I really wouldn't have the will power to turn down an invitation to lunch."

Derek looked at Sam, his eyes full of amusement, and shrugged. "Don't . . . don't you have to get to the office yourself?" Sam asked.

"Oh, no. There's not a thing for me to do there today. I mean, unless you don't *want* me to stay . . ."

Sam thought wryly, Well, at least it'll keep her away from Derek. She smiled and said, "If you can stay for lunch I'd enjoy it, Gloria. Please do."

"Wonderful," Gloria said. They had reached the terrace, and she sat down in a chaise longue. "I'll just wait here while you change. I believe that suit is a trifle skimpier than you're used to—you're getting a little burned around the edges."

At the door to her bedroom, Derek kissed Sam's lips lightly. "I've got to leave in a hurry, little one, and probably won't be back till late. I hate leaving you. . . ."

Sam reached up to trace the line of his lips with a forefinger. "I'll be here, Derek," she said softly.

Sam showered quickly, then pulled on a pair of jeans and a long-sleeved shirt. The air had turned cooler with the approach of the storm that had been threatening all day.

When she went into the dining room, Gloria was on her way in from the terrace. "It looks like we're going to catch it this afternoon," she said. "I wish it would rain and get it over with."

"Hmm. Well, let's have lunch, shall we?" Sam said. She would be glad when Gloria left, when she could be alone with her memories of this morning. Derek

. . . she hadn't had a chance to tell him how much she loved him.

Gloria was quiet at lunch, making several false starts, as if there was a subject she wanted to discuss, but didn't know how to broach it. For her part, Sam kept the conversation impersonal, asking questions about the business.

After lunch, Sam hoped Gloria would leave immediately, but she said, "Let's take our tea out to the porch and have a nice long talk, Sam. All right?"

Sam felt she had no choice but to agree. They were just settled when Gloria said, "Oh, darn! I've spilled tea on this blouse," rubbing at the white silk. "I'd better go wash it off. Don't get up, Sam. I know where the bathroom is."

Sam watched her hurry from the room and sighed. The storm seemed to have stalled in the distance, always threatening, never arriving.

After a few moments Gloria returned and sat down, tucking her green skirt primly around her knees. There was a light in her eyes that made Sam uneasy. "That's very bright of you, Sam, having your own room. I mean, under the circumstances."

Sam leaned forward and set her iced tea carefully on the table in front of her, giving herself time to compose her face. Then she looked coolly at the redhead. "Did you lose your way searching for the bathroom, Gloria?"

The green eyes widened in mock innocence. "I just happened to turn in the wrong direction. But I do think it's smart. You must have heard about Derek's reputation."

Sam forced herself to meet Gloria's stare levelly. "What are you talking about, Gloria? If you're making some sort of insinuation about my husband—"

Gloria waved a hand airily, and sipped her tea.

"Oh, that. Well, everyone knows Derek is quite a ladies' man. But in your situation, you have to protect yourself, don't you? I mean since the marriage is just a sham—"

Sam pretended indignation, her loyalty to Derek telling her she must fool Gloria. He had said it was important that no one know the truth about their marriage. "A sham! Now listen, Gloria, I don't know what you're talking about, but I'm losing patience with you."

"I tell you it's all right, Sam—you don't need to pretend with me. Derek told me all about it. He married you because in order to inherit, under his father's will, he has to be married."

"His father's will?" Sam said weakly. Is that what this was all about—a scheme to inherit money?

Gloria leaned forward, her face full of sincerity. "Yes, of course. Surely you knew? Of course you did. And for some people—people like Derek—under the circumstances, well, you *are* married. But I can tell that you take things too seriously for that, Sam. That's why I said it was smart of you to have your own bedroom. Don't get me wrong, Derek's a great guy, and wonderful to work for, as well as—well, never mind that. But the thing is, you just can't take him too seriously."

Sam laughed harshly. "That's strange. Someone used those exact words the other day, only they were talking about you."

If Sam had hoped to embarrass Gloria, she was disappointed. The redhead laughed delightedly. "That would be Jeff, right?" She shook her head. "Poor Jeff, he's one of the serious ones, like you. He's right—I admit it freely. I think life is for living, not for waiting to live. Derek and I are alike that way."

Sam swallowed, fighting back a growing nausea,

and made another effort. "Gloria, I insist that you not make any more disparaging remarks about my husband—who *is* my husband, by the way. I don't know where you've gotten this strange idea that our marriage is a sham, or this business about a will—"

"The will is a matter of public record, Sam. Seems Derek was quite a playboy in his younger days, and since his wife's death too. His father wanted him to settle down, and that's why he set the will up so that Derek had to be married to inherit." She waved a slender hand at the room. "You think this kind of living comes cheap? And Derek likes the plushest home, the fastest cars, and the most beautiful women."

Sam felt her face paling. Surely this couldn't be true. "You're making this up, Gloria. You wanted Derek yourself, so—"

Gloria laughed with every indication of hearty enjoyment. "I had Derek, and still do—grow up, Sam! Oh, not to marry—but I never wanted to marry him. I don't want to marry a man who can never be happy with just one woman. All Derek and I wanted from each other was what we got. But then my needs are earthier than yours, Sam. As for making anything up—I suspected it for days, ever since that oh, so sudden wedding, but Derek admitted it to me while we were in Atlanta. So I don't have to make anything up about your marriage—I know the truth."

Sam's hand went to her throat, Gloria's last words driving the others from her mind. "You . . . you were in Atlanta with him?"

Gloria laughed again, and stood to leave. "How long has it been since you left the farm, Sam? This is the big city." At the doorway she turned. "A final word of warning: The one thing Derek loves above all is a challenge, especially when it involves a beautiful woman, and I'll give you that—you're beautiful. I just hope you're smart, too."

"Derek loves me," Sam said defiantly, in spite of the trembling that shook her body.

"Oh, please," Gloria said, rolling her eyes. "He *always* says that, Sam. If it's necessary." And she left.

Sam slumped back on the wicker couch, staring with unseeing eyes at the purple clouds above the ocean. Gloria was wrong—she had to be. She was simply a spite-filled secretary who had hoped to marry the boss, striking out in anger. And yet . . .

There had to be a reason for the pretence of a marriage. When Derek had hired her, he had said he needed to be married for legal reasons. She remembered that day so vividly. He must have meant what Gloria claimed: that he needed a wife in order to inherit under his father's will.

But Derek—Sam's eyes clouded as she thought of the Derek she knew—or had believed she knew. A man who didn't care overmuch for material things, who loved the ocean, and his daughter—and Sam. But Gloria was right—Derek did live well. Sam thought of the Mercedes, the expensive hotels in Atlanta and Puerto Rico. Could it be her nightmares had been a warning—a warning that Derek was indeed very much like Kyle?

Sam walked over to the windows, pacing nervously. She's right, she thought miserably. Gloria has to be right. How could she know the marriage was a pretence unless Derek had told her? And if he told her that, he must have told her the reason as well.

When they were in Atlanta he told her, Sam thought with a fresh pang. She had gone with him! He had asked Sam to go to Atlanta with him, and when she couldn't . . . She laid her face against the cool window frame, feeling tears burn her eyes.

And today— The blood rushed to Sam's cheeks and she beat her fist softly against the back of a wicker chair. If Gloria hadn't shown up when she did . . .

Was the redhead right about that as well? Was Sam simply a challenge to Derek? No! something inside her cried. He loved her!

Gloria's words seemed to echo in the room, replying: He always says that—if it's necessary.

Sam was relieved when the doorbell rang, shattering her thoughts. She hoped it was Trudy returning. She needed someone to talk to, to help her sort out lies from truth.

It was Jeff Templeton. She made an effort to sound happy to see him, but his dark eyes were grave, searching her face. She was sure he realized she had been crying. Sam seated him on the sunporch and went to get iced tea, glad of the opportunity to cover the traces of her weeping. She still had her pride. There was no point in letting the world know how badly she had been hurt.

She sat down on the sofa beside Jeff and handed him a glass of tea. "Well!" she said cheerfully. "A few minutes earlier, and you could have visited with Gloria as well."

"Really? Too bad I missed her," Jeff said, with no trace of disappointment in his voice. "I haven't seen her in days."

"Oh?"

"No. She's been . . . out of town." Sam thought there was a trace of embarrassment in his voice. She looked into her glass to hide the tears that threatened. It seemed Jeff knew Gloria had been in Atlanta with Derek.

Jeff hurried on, in an obvious attempt to change the subject, to tell Sam about the work he was doing in Jacksonville, and how anxious he was to get home to Georgia. Finally he stopped in some confusion and touched Sam's hand.

"Sam, if you ever . . . need a friend, a . . . a shoulder to cry on—I'm a good listener."

Sam turned her head to look out the window. Oh, please, she begged silently, don't be so kind or I'll start crying and never be able to stop! After a moment she looked back at Jeff, forcing a smile. "I wouldn't want to monopolize your time, Jeff."

"Why not?" he asked gently. "I can't think of a better way to spend it."

The earnestness of his tone made Sam suddenly uncomfortable. "Well . . . I don't think Gloria would like it if you spent all your time listening to my problems while you're in town."

"Gloria has nothing to say about how I spend my time, Sam."

"Oh, Jeff, I'm sorry. I didn't mean to . . ." Again Sam was reminded of the teenager who had a crush on her, and fumbled for words.

He laughed shortly. "Look, as I told you before, I knew Gloria in high school. When I found out I was going to be here in town for some time, I decided to look her up, and I'll admit I was pretty interested in her. But it didn't take me long to find out that she was already involved with—" He stopped.

"With Derek," Sam said flatly. It was true, then.

"Oh, hell. Sam, I'm sorry. Look, I may be wrong. I . . . don't know for sure . . ."

He looked so unhappy that Sam wanted to spare his feelings. "It's all right, Jeff. I already know—that is, I just found out today."

He grasped her shoulders. "Sam, is there anything I can do?"

Sam shook her head, feeling tears begin in spite of everything she could do to hold them back.

"Listen," Jeff said eagerly, "now that Derek's married, Gloria will back off. I'm sure this thing started before he knew you. It'll be all right, Sam. Like I told you before, you're worth ten Glorias, and Derek loves you."

The sob was involuntary, and when Jeff pulled her into his arms she accepted his comforting gratefully. "No, he doesn't," she wept against his suit jacket. "He doesn't love me, Jeff. He just . . ."

"Just what, Sam?" he asked gently.

She shook her head, the sobs racking her body.

Jeff patted her back awkwardly. "Of course he loves you. He married you."

This brought a fresh torrent. I can't lie anymore, Sam thought. Anyway, what difference did it make? He hadn't thought twice about telling Gloria! "That doesn't mean anything. He . . . he just married me because his father's will says he has to be married to inherit!"

Jeff was very still for a moment, not speaking. Then he said, "Now, Sam, you're imagining things. What makes you think that's why Derek married you? Did he admit that?"

Something had crept into his voice that Sam didn't like at all—something calculating. She looked up at him through her tears, a warning clamoring in her mind. What have I done? it cried. Aloud she said, "Well, no. But if he loved me, he wouldn't have taken Gloria to Atlanta with him."

Strange, that mixture of sincerity and adoration seemed missing from Jeff's brown eyes at the moment, having been replaced by a light of curiosity.

"But what makes you think his father's will is involved in this, Sam?"

"I . . . Jeff, really . . ."

"After all," he said, not giving her time to think, "didn't you and Derek practically fall in love at first sight?" Sam started as she realized that, for her part anyway, that was true. If only Derek . . .

"And then there was that famous whirlwind courtship and marriage in Atlanta, right?" Jeff was saying. "So why do you have doubts about his feelings, and so soon? You've only been married a couple of weeks."

"Of course we have. But . . . really, Jeff, you make me feel as if I'm on the witness stand," Sam said.

He laughed shortly and ran a hand through his sandy hair. "I'm sorry, Sam. I just hate to see you so unhappy."

"We'll work it out, Jeff. As you say, we've only been married a couple of weeks. I . . . I didn't mean what I said, I was just angry to find that Gloria had gone to Atlanta. I shouldn't have been. She *is* his secretary, and I'm sure there was a good reason for her to accompany him." She smiled at him coaxingly. "Please just chalk this up to newlywed insecurity, okay?"

He smiled. "Well, okay. But I still don't understand why you—" He broke off as Debby ran into the room.

"Hey, Sam, wait'll you see the neat stuff Aunt Trudy got me!" she exclaimed before she saw Jeff.

Stifling a sigh of relief, Sam introduced Jeff to Debby, and to Trudy, who followed a moment later. Jeff talked to them for a very few minutes, seeming eager to leave.

Then Sam *did* sigh heavily, and Trudy's sharp eyes took in every detail—from Sam's red-rimmed eyes to the hopeless slump of her body against the cushions of the sofa. "Debby," the older woman said, "it's hot out and we've had a hard day shopping.

Why don't you take a nice shower and let Sam and me talk for a few minutes? Then you can model your new clothes for her."

When Debby left the sunporch, Trudy sat down beside Sam and held out her arms wordlessly. Sam fell into them like a hurt child, sobbing. It was some minutes before she quieted, and accepted the tissues Trudy dug from her capacious handbag.

"Now," Trudy said calmly, "tell me."

"So much has happened, I . . . I don't know where to begin. Derek came home this morning, Trudy."

"He left Atlanta early. Doesn't that tell you how much he loves you?" Trudy interposed.

"Wait—he said he loved me, and—" Sam stopped as the tears filled her voice once more. "Trudy, I love him so! But . . . anyway, I didn't have a chance to tell him. We . . . we were . . . swimming, and—I didn't get to tell him I love him . . ."

"Why not?" she asked gently.

"Gloria showed up. She said he was needed at the office. Somebody insisted on seeing him."

"Drat that woman! If it were up to me—anyway, there must be more than this to get you so upset. What happened?"

Sam looked at Trudy, ignoring the tears that streamed down her cheeks, and said, "Trudy, why didn't you tell me Derek wanted the marriage so he could inherit under his father's will? Why did you let me think he loved me when you knew Gloria went with him to Atlanta, that they were . . . lovers?"

The older woman sprang back, her face white. "What!"

"I know all about it. Gloria told me. And apparently Derek told her about our marriage agreement while they were in Atlanta together."

Trudy laid a hand on her wrist. "Now, wait a

minute, Sam. Let me think. I've got to figure out what G.G. is up to."

Sam made an impatient gesture. "Seems pretty simple to me. I've been a gullible fool."

"Now stop that! If you believe anything that woman says, you *are* gullible." She stopped for a moment, her eyes narrowed. "Hmm. Well, let's start with the trip to Atlanta. There's no question about that one. G.G.'s been in the office all week."

"You mean she lied? But Jeff said she was out of town, too."

"Maybe she lied to him, too, Sam. I don't know about that, but I *do* know I've had the pleasure of Miss Lanahan's company—dubious as it is—all week in the office."

Sam tried to fight the feeling of relief that made her head spin, but felt a smile trembling at the corners of her mouth.

"Better, huh?" Trudy said slyly. She stood up and walked over to the windows. She looked out, tapping her foot, then sighed. She returned to the sofa beside Sam. "Look, I probably shouldn't do this— Derek would be furious. But after the line G.G. fed you this afternoon—I think it would be better for you to know the truth about why Derek hired you."

"Gloria told me, Trudy. Because of his father's will."

Trudy sighed. "No, child," she said patiently. "That was another of her lies. Or maybe she believes that, but Derek certainly didn't tell her that, because that's not the way it was." She leaned back against the sofa and took off her shoes. "I believe we walked through every department store in Jacksonville today," she said, rubbing her feet.

"Trudy, please," Sam said, leaning forward urgently.

Trudy smiled tiredly. "Okay, Sam. It is true that

Tom Spencer had a provision in his will that Derek must be married before he inherited—he's the only heir. But that was put in there long before Derek ever married Vicky, back in his young—and, yes, slightly wild—days. Ned Palmer has already told Derek there won't be any problem about that. I believe he has something from Tom authorizing a change—I don't know. But it's not important."

"Then why—"

"It all goes back to Vicky," Trudy said, sighing. "When she and Derek first married, he adored her. And Debby—he loved the child to distraction. Then when things went sour, Vicky took the child and went to live with her parents. I don't know what Vicky told them about Derek, but she wasn't the type to be particularly fair."

Trudy shook her head, remembering. "She was spoiled. An only child, her parents couldn't say no to her, and when she died—they convinced Derek it would be better for Debby to stay with them a while."

"Yes, Derek told me that much," Sam said.

"Well, every time he suggested that Debby come back home, they found a reason to put it off. Finally he went up there for a visit one weekend. They live in Georgia. He was pretty upset when he got back."

"Why? What was wrong?"

"To begin with, he had the feeling they were using Debby . . . to take Vicky's place as their daughter. And he could see that they were spoiling her as they had Vicky. Her grades were bad, there was no discipline—the child made her own rules," Trudy said, shaking her head once more.

"That's not good," Sam said, remembering her father's rules, how even when she had resented them they had made her feel cherished.

"No," Trudy agreed firmly, "it's not." Her face

softened. "She's like a different little girl here with you and Derek, Sam."

Sam smiled at Trudy. "But what does this have to do with—"

Trudy sighed again. "Derek finally set a date and told Vicky's parents he wanted Debby home by that time, or else. Well, they sent her home, all right, but they also threatened to go to court, to try to get custody of Debby. Derek thinks they will, and he didn't want his bachelor status to be a point against him."

"You mean that's why he hired me?" Sam said, staring at Trudy.

"That's why. Ned told him he'd probably win custody anyway, but he didn't want to leave anything to chance where Debby was involved. That's why he was so concerned that no one know the truth about your marriage."

Sam frowned. "But how did Gloria figure it out if Derek didn't tell her?"

Trudy sighed. "Sam, that's typical of her. She's the biggest snoop in the world, and when Derek was interviewing you that first day, and then had Ned come down with the contract, you'd better believe Miss Lanahan was all ears. You didn't let her know how close she came, did you?"

"No, I didn't admit—oh, no—Jeff," Sam whispered, her face paling.

"What is it, Sam?"

"Jeff came by right after Gloria left. Oh, Trudy, I think I've made a terrible mistake," Sam wailed. "If I had only had time—but he caught me when I was still trying to understand it all—"

Trudy patted her hand. "Now, come on, Sam. How bad is it? What did you tell him?"

"That Gloria had gone to Atlanta with Derek—but

Jeff already believed that himself, so that doesn't matter. But, Trudy, I told him that Derek didn't love me—that he just married me because of his father's will." Sam pressed her hand to her mouth, as if she could still recall the words. If only she could! she thought.

Trudy took a deep breath. "You told him exactly that? Did you tell him it was a business deal, with a contract?"

"No, but—"

"Well, it might not be so bad then. It might have sounded as if you and Derek had had a spat, and you were just making accusations. It's not great, Sam, but it could have been worse."

Sam searched the older woman's face. "Do you think maybe it wasn't too bad? I did try to smooth it over as insecurity on my part—" She stopped, remembering the moment when she had become cautious. "He was awfully interested, Trudy. I even felt he was . . . I don't know . . . giving me the third degree."

Trudy said, "Well, it's too late to worry about it now, Sam. Could be he's just nosy, like Gloria. Anyhow, didn't you say he'd be going back to Georgia soon?"

Sam nodded. "I think I'd better tell Derek about it, though. I'm afraid he's going to be pretty angry, but . . ."

"Oh, he'll be mad, okay, but I think you should tell him. Besides," she grinned, "I have a feeling Derek's never going to be able to stay angry with you for very long."

"I hope not," Sam said. Then a smile slowly spread across her face. "Gloria really was in the office all week, Trudy?"

Trudy smiled indulgently. "Yes, Samantha, dear. All week."

"So she lied about being in Atlanta with Derek, and about the reason he wanted to be married. That means she probably lied about . . . all of it."

"About their being lovers?" Trudy asked. "I can't say about the time when they went out together some, but I doubt it. As for now—if they're lovers I'll turn in my junior G-man badge and tear up my application for private detective school!"

Sam inspected a fingernail carefully as she spoke. "Trudy, Gloria also said Derek was . . . well, a sort of scalp collector. I mean, you know, with women?"

Trudy hooted. "And that's what's bothering you? Oh, Sam!" Seeing Sam's face, she sobered. "Look, child, maybe he was years ago, before he married Vicky. But he was awful young then. I think Vicky just about cured him of women forever. I was beginning to think he was totally immune, until you came along. No, Sam, that's just another of G.G.'s fantasies. Or wishful thinking on her part." she snorted.

Sam felt a smile broaden into a grin, then she and Trudy were giggling together like schoolgirls. Debby came into the room in a new school dress to begin the fashion show, and soon was caught up in contagious glee she didn't understand, but enjoyed thoroughly.

Nine

Derek wasn't home by dinnertime, and Sam and Debby ate alone. Debby talked happily about her new clothes, and about school starting in a couple of weeks. The storm had finally arrived, and Sam glanced out the windows and then at her watch, nervously. Lightning flashes illuminated the sky, and Tiptoe, wet and indignant, came hurrying through the kitchen when Mrs. Holmes opened the door. He settled himself on the dining room floor, close to Sam's feet, to lick away the raindrops.

The rain continued through the evening. Sam went to her room and got ready for bed, still looking at her watch often. Well, Derek had said he might be late.

She tried to read in bed, but her mind kept mulling over the events of the day. This morning, in the cove with Derek . . . Her face softened, remembering. If only Gloria hadn't shown up, we might be together now, she thought. But there's time, all the time in the world.

Sam frowned, angry with herself. If only she hadn't been so quick to believe Gloria—she should have known Gloria was lying. And Jeff. Now she had to tell Derek about that. Please, oh please, she thought, don't let me have done any harm to his chances of getting custody of Debby!

She finally fell asleep, listening for the sound of Derek's car in the drive.

Sam was up early the next morning, and looked out the sliding glass doors to see a clear sky, the air fresh after the storm of the night before. She took a shower and dressed quickly, anxious to see Derek. She had just slipped her feet into sandals when there was a knock on the connecting door.

"Come in," she called, surprised to find her voice shook.

He strode into the room. Sam's smile froze midway, at the expression on his face. "Derek, what—?"

Scowling briefly in her direction, he walked to the dresser and pulled out the drawers, dumping the contents on her bed. "Derek, what are you doing?" Sam cried.

He stopped, hands on hips, and looked at her with eyes of ice. "You're moving," he said. "Into my room. *Our* room."

Five minutes before, Sam would have found this suggestion more than a little agreeable—but not like this. "Are you so sure—"

She stopped abruptly as he advanced on her, towering over her. He didn't touch her, only looked down at her, forcing her to lean her head back to meet his eyes—eyes in which danger lurked. "Yes?" he said coldly. "You had a question?" There was challenge in his manner, but not his usual mockery, with laughter just beneath the surface. No, this time there was something that frightened her in his anger.

When she continued to stare at him silently, he turned and emptied the last drawer on the bed, then pulled off the bedspread, carrying the bundle into his room. Sam followed him, open-mouthed.

"I've emptied the top two drawers of my dresser," he said, dropping the things on his bed. "You can have those."

"Derek, I don't understand," Sam said. "I—"

He turned to her, the heat flashing in his eyes a strange contrast to the controlled coldness of his voice. "Then maybe I'd better explain it to you," he said. His hands gripped her shoulders in a painful hold. "I understand you had a visit from your *good* friend Jeff Templeton yesterday afternoon."

"Yes, I wanted to talk to you about that. But how did you—"

He laughed harshly. "How did I know? Well, I'll tell you, Sam. You were aware, of course, that Jeff is a lawyer from Georgia, but I think I'll give you the benefit of the doubt and assume that you didn't know who his clients are."

Sam shook her head. "I don't understand what—"

"His clients are Fred and Agnes Hill, Vicky's parents."

Sam put a hand to her mouth. "Oh, no," she whispered. "Derek, I told—"

His voice was hard. "I know exactly what you told him, Sam. I got it all from Fred on the telephone last night at the office." His grip on her shoulders tightened. "Now you listen to me, I don't care why you told Templeton what you did," he said, and Sam winced at the pain she saw briefly in his eyes. "I finally convinced Fred we had had a newlywed's spat— thank God you didn't bare your soul completely and tell your *friend* about the contract, too." The bitterness in his voice brought tears to Sam's eyes.

"Oh, Derek. I'm so sorry. I had no idea Jeff was working for Vicky's parents."

"I'm sure you didn't," he said, but there was no warmth, no sign of forgiveness, in his voice. "As I said, I convinced Fred it was just a lover's quarrel that made you say what you did. *But* he and Agnes are driving down here today, to see the happy couple for themselves. And you'd better believe, Sam, we're going to be the most sickeningly sweet, lovey-dovey couple they've ever seen."

Sam nodded. "All right, Derek." It was the least she could do, she thought miserably.

He dropped his hands from her shoulders, as if he had no desire to touch her any longer. "By the way, where did you get that baloney about my father's will?"

"Gloria told—"

He waved a hand in disgust. "Never mind, that doesn't matter. I guess you'd better know the truth. I—"

"It's all right, Trudy told me. I know why you wanted to pretend to be married."

"Good," he said tonelessly. "Fred and Agnes will be here this afternoon. They'll leave sometime tomorrow. I want you to get all your things out of the other room and bath. They'll sleep in there, and I don't want so much as a hairpin left to indicate you've been sleeping there."

"Yes—all right." He turned to leave the room. "Derek—"

"What?" he asked, his hand on the door.

"I . . . I'm sorry." Please, she begged silently, please take me in your arms . . .

"I am, too," he said quietly, and left.

For a few minutes Sam stood in Derek's room, tears spilling unheeded from her eyes. Then she brushed them aside, telling herself, Okay, Sam, you did the damage—now get busy helping to *undo* it.

She emptied the cupboard in the bathroom of her cosmetics, took her clothes from the hamper and dropped them in the one in Derek's bath, then carried armloads of clothes from the closet. She rechecked all the dresser drawers, although she couldn't imagine anything being left in them after Derek's efficient, if untidy, method of cleaning them out. Then she lay on her stomach to peer under the bed. When she stood and brushed off her knees, she knew the room contained no traces of her presence.

She put her things away in Derek's bedroom, pushing aside the thought that she would be staying with him there tonight. From his manner toward her a few minutes earlier, she knew this night was not going to be as she had imagined. Well, the important thing just now was to preserve a facade, to convince the Hills that they could make a good home for Debby.

And we could have, too, Sam thought, tears misting her eyes once more. Now what? she wondered. Would Derek be able to forgive her for betraying his confidence in something that was so important to him?

Finished, Sam went out to the living room to find Debby and Derek. "Oh, Sam!" Debby exclaimed. "Daddy thought you were still asleep—we're going to the zoo! Will you come with us? Please, Sam!"

Sam looked at Derek. "Honey, I think Sam has too much to do, with your grandparents coming to visit. Maybe another time," he said easily.

Sam knelt and hugged the child, to hide the pain on her face. Obviously Derek didn't want her company. "Not this time, Deb. You say hello to the bears for me, okay? And tell the tigers their cousin Tiptoe sends greetings."

"Okay," Debby giggled, "I'll tell them. I bet they'd love Tiptoe," she said, walking to the door with her father.

"Yes, for lunch," Sam heard Derek say dryly.

"Daddy!" the little girl chided, as they walked to the car.

Sam closed the door and sighed, wishing the pretence they had to go through with today was real, that she and Derek were loving newlyweds. The three of them could be a happy family . . . but it looked as if she had ruined that.

The morning dragged by, the clear skies giving way to thunderclouds once again. Sam had lunch alone, wondering what she would say to Vicky's parents if Derek wasn't back when they arrived.

She was relieved when the Mercedes pulled into the drive. Debby hurried in to tell Sam all about the zoo. When Derek followed, his face was as grim as before. Only when he spoke to his daughter did the lines of tension around his mouth ease slightly. The three of them sat in the living room, Debby and Sam on the couch, talking, and Derek in the easy chair, hidden behind the morning newspaper. He won't even look at me, Sam thought miserably.

It was late afternoon before the Hills arrived. As Sam had often noticed in couples who had been married for many years, they resembled one another. They were short, plump, and had thick, silver-white hair. Their affection for Debby was obvious; their gray eyes lit up when they talked to her.

Conversation among the adults was somewhat awkward, however. Sam and Derek sat on the sofa in the living room. Derek put an arm around Sam's shoulders as soon as they were seated. This time she didn't flinch at his touch, but it seemed to her that he was reluctant to play his part in the charade now. She forced herself not to think about his reasons, to smile as if they were a happy couple.

Debby's presence prevented them from touching on the purpose of the visit until she went to bed, so dinner was a strained affair. Sam and Derek continued playing their roles, with many smiles across the table at one another. But Sam was painfully aware that Derek's smiles didn't reach his eyes.

Finally it was Debby's bedtime. Fred Hill looked up, surprised, when Derek replied to Debby's protest, "No, I said it's bedtime *now*. You'll be able to see Grandma and Grandpa some more tomorrow. Come kiss your daddy goodnight."

She did so without further argument, then hugged him tightly and said, "I loved the zoo, Daddy. Thank you." Then she kissed her grandparents and Sam goodnight. "Will you come in in a minute, Sam?" she whispered, as if embarrassed by a childish desire to be tucked in. Sam nodded, smiling.

A few minutes later Sam excused herself and went down the hall to Debby's room. The little girl was in bed. Sam sat on the edge of the bed and smoothed a curl back from her face. "Good night, tiger," she said.

Debby giggled. "Oh, Sam." Then she asked, "Do you like my grandma and grandpa? They're nice, aren't they?"

"Yes, they are, Deb. I like them." She waited a moment, sensing the child had more to say.

"I do too. But Sam—I'm glad I'm staying here with you and Daddy. I missed Daddy."

Sam hugged her. "So am I, honey. You go to sleep now, okay?"

Sam left, and met Agnes Hill in the hallway; she had been looking into the room. "Did you want to say goodnight to Debby again?" Sam asked gently. The woman looked on the verge of tears.

She shook her head. "No. That is, I did—but I think not just now." She followed Sam down the hallway to the living room.

Derek rose from the sofa, smiling that awful smile that was so different from the grin she loved. When she sat down beside him once more, he put his arm around her, but she still felt cold with a chill that it seemed would never leave her.

For a few minutes the four of them made more polite, stilted conversation. Then Fred Hill leaned forward and slapped his hands on his knees in a let's-get-down-to-business gesture. "Now look, you all know the reason we came here—"

"Fred, we're all tired. I think we ought to let this go till morning," Agnes said, looking older than her sixty years.

"What? Agnes, I thought you were so anxious to get this cleared up. You said—"

"I know. But I think we should sleep on it, Fred." Her voice was insistent.

For a moment he regarded her in puzzled silence. Then Derek said, "We'll have some time alone in the morning. Trudy is taking Debby to Sunday school."

Agnes rose from her chair. "Good. Then I think we ought to tell these folks goodnight, Fred. We've had a long drive today."

Muttering, shaking his head, Fred followed her down the hall to their room. Derek stood, yawning loudly. "I guess we might as well call it a day, too. Coming, dear?"

Sam looked at him, thinking for a moment she would see the old mocking grin, but there was no laughter in his eyes—only a grim determination to continue the charade.

When they entered his bedroom and closed the door, Sam asked quietly, "Where am I going to sleep, Derek?"

"In my bed," he said, his voice low.

"Then where are you—"

"We're both sleeping in my bed," he interrupted.

"Not like this," she said angrily, and started toward the door. In a flash he was beside her, gripping her arms.

"Now you listen to me," he said through clenched teeth. "Fred and Agnes are right next door. We are going to make this . . . farce as real as possible. There are going to be two people in this room, sleeping in one bed. There is going to be nothing—do you hear me, nothing!—to arouse their suspicions. Do you understand?"

"Yes," she whispered, throat dry.

He released her, and for a moment there was a touch of the old mockery in his voice, but with an edge. "Don't worry, Sam. I'm not playing games—the prize is not half so tempting anymore."

She turned so he couldn't see the tears that sprang to her eyes, and took her football jersey from the drawer. He strode up behind her and pulled it from her hands. "Oh, no, Sam. Not tonight. If there should be a fire, or natural disaster, or whatever, my bride is not going to be seen by the Hills in a football jersey." He pulled out the lacy blue nightgown she had bought at Colette's. "Don't you think this is more appropriate for someone in your . . . shall I say, newly married condition?"

Angela Gadsden

She faced him with fire in her eyes. "Now that's too much. I won't—"

"Then this one," he said, thrusting the sheer black gown at her. "Take your choice. You can have the bath first," he added, walking over to look out at the ocean, "but when you come out, you'd better be wearing one of those two gowns, or I swear I'll put you into one of them myself."

Sam stood speechless, staring at his back, holding the gowns. Then he turned, his eyes covering her from head to foot, and said, "Is that what you want?" He took a step toward her.

"No," she said, tossing the black gown on the bed, taking the blue one into the bathroom with her. When she returned he hardly glanced at her as he went into the bathroom.

Sam got into the king-sized bed and lay as close to the edge as she could. She could hear the shower running for a long time. When the bathroom door opened, she closed her eyes, trembling. She felt the mattress shift as he lay down, and found herself hoping, even now, that he would take her into his arms.

"Goodnight, Samantha," he said coolly.

"Goodnight," she answered against her pillow, to muffle the tears in her voice. She was back to Samantha, she thought, as if he didn't know her anymore.

It seemed hours to Sam that she lay there awake, listening to the rumble of thunder in the distance, but finally she went to sleep.

A loud clap of thunder woke her. For a moment she forgot where she was and enjoyed the sound of rain beating on the windows. Then another loud burst seemed to shake the house. Sam started, and realized she was curled up against Derek. A lump came to her throat as she remembered everything that had happened.

He was asleep, judging by the sound of his breathing. Outside the storm raged. Sam had always been nervous when lightning flashed, and even though he was angry and cold toward her, she found Derek's presence comforting. She inched closer to him until her face was resting against his broad back, cuddling close to his warmth.

He stirred in his sleep, pressing closer against her, and involuntarily her body arched to fit the contours of his back. She heard the change in his breathing and lay still, heart pounding. When he turned and propped himself up on an elbow to look at her, she didn't pretend to be asleep, but met his eyes. A flash of lightning showed her his face, a muscle working in his jaw. "What are you doing, Sam?" he asked harshly. "Dammit, is this what you want?" He pulled her to him and claimed her mouth roughly.

Yes, she thought, yes, this is what I want. The touch of his lips triggered all the new sensations that only Derek had ever aroused in her. She wanted to tell him again and again how much she loved him, but he wouldn't release her mouth. His hands were on her body with a roughness that surprised her, ripping her gown.

Not like this, Derek, she longed to say, but when she tried to speak he thrust his tongue between her parted lips. She struggled to push him away, but he gripped her wrists in one strong hand and pulled them over her head.

No! she screamed inwardly, as his other hand pulled her gown up over her thighs. Not like this— this is just like Kyle! It's useless to struggle, she thought, and the tears began—hopeless, silent tears.

Lightning flashed again, and Derek looked at her face. His eyes widened, and he drew back from her. For a moment something like pain twisted his mouth, then he laughed harshly. "Don't worry, Sam. Rape's never appealed to me. There are too many willing partners around. Only spare me the frightened act, please. You weren't so frightened with Templeton."

"Templeton—what do you mean?" Sam asked numbly, not caring. Just like Kyle, just like Kyle, the refrain beat in her mind.

"Forget it," he said disgustedly. "I've had enough lies for one day." He turned over and pounded the pillow. "Do me the favor of keeping your tempting— but useless—little body on your own side of the bed, will you?"

Sam felt drained of tears, and of hope, empty. She lay dry-eyed, waiting for morning. —

Ten

She woke to find Derek, fully dressed, shaking her. "Come on, Sam," he said evenly. "Trudy has taken Debby to Sunday school, and Mrs. Holmes has breakfast ready for the four of us. Showtime, so slip on your happy-bride smile," he finished bitterly.

Sam showered and applied makeup to the purple smudges under her eyes. When she joined Derek and the Hills in the dining room, she looked crisp and cool in a navy silk blouse and pink slacks, showing no trace of the despair she felt.

Mrs. Holmes had made apple pancakes, but for Sam they might have been sawdust. She had no appetite, but forced a few mouthfuls for the sake of appearances. Glancing around the table, she saw that the other three were only picking at their food, as well.

Finally Fred Hill pushed his plate away and said, "Look, Derek, there's no point in dragging this thing out. Agnes and I have decided—" He stopped and glanced at his wife. She nodded, and Sam could see that she had been crying.

"We've decided that Debby would be better off staying with you," Fred concluded. He wiped his mouth with a napkin, as if to get rid of the taste of his words.

Derek looked at both of them, shocked. "Fred—Agnes, are you sure? I mean, that's great, but I thought you . . ." He stopped, and half-smiled at them, not believing it was really this simple.

Agnes smiled, and said in a voice that trembled slightly, "It's better for a child to have young parents, Derek. I know we were upset by Jeff's phone call yesterday, but it's obvious he was mistaken. Anyone could look at you and Sam and know how much you love each other."

Sam met Derek's eyes briefly, and looked away. That much is true, she thought, at least for me. But I'll just have to get over it.

Derek looked miserable. "Agnes," he said, "Sam and I—" and Sam thought, He's going to tell her the truth! After all the lies and pretence . . . She looked at him unbelievingly.

Fred broke in. "Listen, Derek. It's great that you've married again, and we can see that Debby loves Sam," he said, smiling at Sam. "But what really made us decide is the change in Debby. She's turned from a whining, demanding child into a happy, well-behaved one. It hurts to admit that, but . . ."

Agnes nodded. "We know we spoiled Vicky, Derek. And we've just found out in recent months some things—well, things you were too kind to tell us about our daughter." She sighed. "And I guess we were beginning to spoil Debby in the same way. You're doing a better job of raising her than we could," she said, pulling a handkerchief from her purse, wiping her eyes.

Fred nodded. "Her place is with you, Derek. You're her father."

Agnes took a deep breath and said, "Besides, from what I heard last night, when Sam was tucking her in, it's where Debby wants to be." She laughed ruefully. "Maybe the child is wiser than the grown-ups."

Derek looked at Sam, his eyes full of gratitude. That's what she'd remember, she thought, knowing she had to leave soon, and try to pick up the pieces of her life. Forget the coldness of his anger, forget last night's Kyle-like brutality, and remember that she helped him get his daughter back.

"There is one thing we wanted to ask, Derek," Fred said. "Agnes and I have decided to do some traveling, maybe even go around the world. We're planning on being gone for quite a while, maybe as long as a year, so we won't be seeing Debby. It's still over a week till school starts. Do you think—"

"You want her to come back with you for a visit now, Fred?" Derek asked.

"Yes, if you don't think—"

"I think it's a good idea," Derek said, his eyes full of sympathy. "And I know Debby will love it."

Agnes Hill looked at Derek tearfully. "Thank you," she said. Then she smiled and added, "Maybe that will give you two a chance to take a longer honeymoon."

Sam had to force yet another smile at these words, and saw that Derek had no taste for the game any longer, either. Then, incredibly, Agnes continued, "We know there's something wrong between you, though you're very much in love, but—well, Debby's still better off with her own father . . . and you."

The rest of the morning passed in a haze for Sam. Debby got home from Sunday school and was overjoyed to find she was going back with her grandparents for a visit. Sam was relieved not to have Derek slipping an unloving arm about her shoulders in pretended affection any longer.

Sam gave Debby an extra hard good-bye hug, wondering if she would be there to greet her when the child returned. No matter what happens, they could still be friends, she thought.

When they were gone Sam walked tiredly out to the terrace and sat down. She should be packing, she thought. She couldn't stay here now.

She looked around as Derek pulled a chair up beside her. "Well, it's over," he said, his voice reflecting the weariness she felt.

She nodded. "Yes. All the lies, the pretence—all unnecessary." And if he had known that, he wouldn't have hired me. Would that have been better? *Is* it better to have loved and lost . . . No, it hurts too much.

"Sam," he said softly. "It wasn't a waste. You heard what Fred and Agnes said, about the change in Debby. I think you were responsible for a lot of that change."

She waited a moment till she could speak evenly. "Thank you for that, Derek. If I helped—well, I'm glad."

"Is there . . . anything you wanted to say to me?" he asked, his eyes grave.

What, Derek? she thought. What did he want her to tell him? That she loved him so much she might never get over it? That for a short, glorious time she'd thought they could be happy? That now she knew they couldn't, because of something in her— something that attracted brutal men, men like Kyle— and him.

Aloud she said, "No, nothing," not noticing the pain that flashed in his eyes.

"Nothing about Jeff Templeton?" he asked coldly.

"Jeff's not important," she said dully, closing her eyes against the icy blue of his gaze.

"Well, I'll be leaving then," he said tonelessly. "I'm all packed."

"Leaving?" Sam looked up at him.

"Yes. I still have business to finish in Atlanta." His mouth twisted. "I left with such . . . eagerness on Friday morning that I postponed some meetings, so I have to get back."

Sam remembered his eagerness, and her own. She could feel again the way her heart leapt when she had paused in her swim and seen Derek on the beach. Not trusting her voice, she simply nodded.

When she heard the sliding door to his bedroom close behind him, she let the tears flow, covering her face with her hands. The Mercedes roared down the drive, muffling her sobs.

She went into the bedroom and fell on the bed, Derek's bed. It seemed she could smell his warm, masculine scent. His robe lay across the chair. Everywhere there were traces of him, and Sam knew she couldn't stay there any longer.

She'd go back to Hollyville, she decided. In a few days she'd pack her things and move back into her apartment, but for now—she couldn't stand to be here a moment longer than she had to.

She tossed clothes into a suitcase, hardly looking at them, and told Mrs. Holmes she would be out of town for a few days. The housekeeper assured her she would see that Tiptoe was fed, and in a few minutes Sam was in her little green Rabbit, headed for Tennessee.

*   *   *

It was late when she arrived, but her father was still up. He was so delighted to see her, his greeting so kind, that she burst into tears of relief. The lying was over at last, and she told her father the truth about her marriage to Derek.

She could see that he understood the things she didn't say as well, that he knew she loved Derek. Then, without meaning to, she found herself talking about Kyle, telling her father about the brutal man she had married. It was as if she were starved for honesty, after living so long with lies.

Her father sat quietly, holding her hands, as she finished. "Sam, I wish you could have told me, honey. Maybe I could have helped." He shook his head. "I feel responsible, the way I pushed you and Kyle together . . ."

"No, Dad. You mustn't feel that way. I'm the only one who's responsible for my happiness," she said, realizing suddenly that the words she spoke to comfort him were true.

There was pride in his smile. "You've grown up a lot, Sam. And I can tell you from a father's point of view, what you did for Derek—helping him keep his daughter with him—that's no small thing, honey."

It was almost dawn when Sam went to bed in her old room, and fell into a deep, dreamless sleep.

She spent Monday and Tuesday visiting old friends and enjoying her father's uncritical company. It was good to be around people who smiled without mockery, and she closed her mind to thoughts of Derek.

Tuesday night was her father's regular penny ante poker night, and Sam insisted he go. She turned on the television and found nothing she wanted to watch, and decided to pick up some paperbacks at the drugstore.

She browsed for a while, selecting two new novels, then some lip gloss to go with her deeper tan. She decided against a milkshake, thinking, I don't believe that pink bikini would stand for it!

When she got home, she was humming. She went into the kitchen through the dark, familiar living room and cut a slice of cheese. Atta girl, Sam, she told herself. Much more sensible than a milkshake.

She dropped the knife in the sink. Carrying the cheese and the novels, she turned toward the living room. Kyle stood in the doorway.

"Kyle!" she gasped. "What are you doing here? And how did you get in?"

His smile was as she remembered it, a kind of smirk. He held up a key, letting it dangle from his fingertips. "I used to be a member of the family, remember? Anyhow, what kind of greeting is that for your husband?"

"You're not my husband anymore," she said, dropping the cheese and the books on the table, folding her arms protectively over her thin cotton blouse.

He leaned his lanky frame against the door nonchalantly and laughed. "So I hear. I hear little Sam's moved up in the world. Married to a millionaire, aren't you?"

The light gleamed on his blond hair, but Sam couldn't see any trace of the young man who had won her father's affection and trust—and for a time, her own. "Kyle, I don't have anything to say to you. Why don't you leave?"

He walked toward her with a kind of swagger, taking his time. "Like I said, is that any kind of greeting? Even you used to do better than that, Sam." He thrust an arm around her waist, and planted a short, hard kiss on her lips. She pulled back, wiping her hand across her mouth.

"You haven't changed, have you, Sam?" he jeered. "Maybe I'd better send your new husband a wedding gift—an electric blanket to keep his bed warm."

She walked away from him to stand by the sink. "Get out of here, Kyle!" she cried, her loathing and the beginning of fear making the words tumble out.

He followed her, trapping her in the corner between the sink and the breakfast bar. "I ran into your father today, Sam. Seems you've been telling him all about mean old Kyle, is that right?"

She drew as far away from him as she could, backing up against the sink. "I told him about our marriage, yes."

He rested his hands on the countertop, one on either side of her, so that she couldn't move without touching him. His gray eyes caught hers, and something was building in them, something she still saw in nightmares.

"Kyle, please . . ."

"Still the same scared little rabbit, aren't you, Sam?" he said. "Well, I always knew how to handle you anyhow, didn't I?" He pulled her to him brutally, crushing her till she felt she couldn't breathe. His mouth was hard, punishing, as full of hate as the man himself.

Sam fought him, but he was strong. He ripped the thin cotton shirt. She tried to scream, and he twisted his hand in her hair, saying, "Don't scream, or I'll *really* hurt you." His other hand kneaded her breasts painfully.

She sobbed, gasping for air, the tears blinding her. At the sight of her weeping he smiled, and she remembered it was always better for him when she cried. Suddenly she thought of Derek, of his tenderness when he made love to her, and that last time— even when he was furious with her, there was none of the cruelty that was so much a part of Kyle. How could she have ever thought they were alike?

With that realization the dead feeling that had been a weight in her heart for days was gone, and in its place was rage. "No!" she screamed, not in fear, but in fury.

Kyle drew back slightly. This was a Samantha he had never seen. "Get away from me, Kyle. You know I don't want this," she said in a tightly controlled voice.

He tried to resume his old jaunty air, but this time Sam felt no fear. "Come on, Sam, baby. It's not my fault you're frigid."

"Frigid!" she spat out the word. "No, Kyle, no— that's not the way it was, ever. It was rape, wasn't it? Maybe not technically, but psychologically—it was always rape. That's what you wanted. You didn't want a passionate wife. You wanted—" she laughed shortly "—a scared little rabbit. Well, I'm not scared anymore."

"Oh, no?" he said silkily, then grabbed her again. With one arm he held her body tightly against him while the other tore at the zipper on her jeans. He bent his head to her breasts, biting a nipple painfully.

Sam groped in the sink behind her and found the knife. She brought it around his back and touched the blade to the base of his skull. "Kyle, do you feel that? It's a knife. If you don't take your hands off me this second, I swear I'll kill you," she said quietly.

He drew a sharp breath, then dropped his hands to his sides and stood very still. His face was white. "All right, Sam," he said in a trembling voice. "Don't do anything silly."

"Back up," she said, holding her hands aside to let him move. He did as she said, slowly. She brought the knife around to hold it between them, with both hands.

"Now get out," she said. He turned to go. "Kyle," she said.

"Yes?" She could see the perspiration on his forehead and upper lip, and knew that like all bullies, he was a coward.

"Leave the key to the house on the table. You won't need it anymore."

He did as she said, then walked out the door. She heard him stumbling down the steps. Then she ran to the door and locked it, putting on the chain. She slumped to the floor against it, trembling, but elated with new knowledge—the knowledge that she was free of Kyle at last. She might have to live without Derek, but there would be no more nightmares.

Eleven

When Sam's father came out to the kitchen the next morning, he found her sitting at the table with a fresh pot of coffee, her suitcases at the door. He wasn't surprised, but when she explained that she was anxious to get her things moved out of Derek's house and back to her apartment, he said, "Of course," in a very tolerant tone.

Sam looked up to see his eyes twinkling. "Well, I *am* anxious to get settled again," she said defensively.

He put on a look of affronted innocence. "Did I say a word?" He poured himself a cup of coffee and sat down. "But I know my daughter—she's a fighter."

Sam grinned at him. "I've never thought of myself as a fighter, Dad." Then she remembered last night, with Kyle. "Maybe I am, though—and high time, too."

"You always have been, Sam. And if you love Derek, I think you'll fight for him."

She sipped her coffee. "Well, the thought did cross my mind that Derek should be back from Atlanta by now, and it will be late when I get there, so he should be at home. . . . I don't know, Dad. It may be too late to patch things up, but . . . well, I'm going to try."

He raised his cup in a toast. "Good girl. I was beginning to be afraid your marriage to Kyle had taken all the fight out of you."

Sam thought for a moment, then told her father about Kyle's visit the night before. He was shaken and angry about the incident, but Sam put a calming hand on his arm, and said, "Don't you see, Dad? I'm glad it happened. Now I'll never be afraid of him again. I don't have to think about Kyle anymore."

Sam made better time than she expected to on the trip to Jacksonville. Her hopes soared higher with every mile. When she pulled into the driveway at the villa it was only a little after four, and she knew Derek would probably still be at the office.

The house felt strangely empty. She put her suitcases in her old room, smiling as she thought maybe she'd never sleep in that bed again, but with Derek in his room—*their* room.

The kitchen was empty. Then there was a tap at the front door, and Mrs. Holmes called out, "Mrs. Spencer?" Sam went into the living room to find the housekeeper, obviously dressed to go out.

"Why, Mrs. Spencer—I wasn't expecting you. I thought—Phillip and I were just about to leave. Mr. Spencer gave me a week off, just before he left this morning."

"Left?" Sam echoed. "Oh, you mean for the office."

"No—for the airport, I thought. He was on the phone, and said he'd be right over to pick up the tickets. I just assumed when he told me I could take a week off, that you were going to be with him—"

"Did you say tickets—more than one?" Sam asked, hating the thought that was beginning to fill her mind.

"Yes. I—like I said, I thought you were going with him, but I guess it must have been a business associate." Sam glanced at the woman, but her expression was sincere and open. Clearly Mrs. Holmes did not share Sam's suspicions.

She smiled warmly at the housekeeper. "I guess so. Well, thank you, Mrs. Holmes. Are you going on vacation?"

"Well, we were—but if you need me here—"

"Of course not. You have a good time," Sam said. At the door, Mrs. Holmes turned with an uncertain look on her face, but Sam grinned and made a shooing motion, and she left.

When the door closed, Sam's grin faded. Derek had left town—and not alone. Maybe it *was* a business trip, part of her mind asserted, but she had an uneasy feeling that it wasn't.

Sam looked at her watch. Four-thirty. Trudy should still be at the office. She dialed the number, biting her lip as the phone rang. A strange voice answered, "Spencer Industries."

"Could I speak to Trudy Wright, please? This is Sam Spencer."

"She's not here, Mrs. Spencer. May I help you?"

"Who is this, please?" Sam asked.

"I'm Martha Young. I usually work in Filing, but I'm helping Trudy out today."

Sam hesitated. She had hoped Trudy would be able to tell her where Derek was—and who was with him. Well, there was a way to answer one question that nagged at her.

"Could I speak to Gloria Lanahan?"

"I'm sorry. Gloria won't be in the rest of the week."

Sam dropped the telephone back into its cradle with lifeless fingers. That was it then—Gloria had won after all.

You practically threw Derek into her arms, a voice inside her taunted. When he asked you about Jeff Templeton you didn't even bother to explain how you happened to confide in him. What did you expect Derek to think? So now he's put you out of his life and flown off with Gloria.

The phone rang. Maybe it's Derek! Sam thought, rushing to answer it, but it was Mrs. Holmes. She wanted to let Sam know that Trudy was keeping Tiptoe while she and Phillip were gone.

"I was afraid you'd be worried about him, Mrs. Spencer."

"Thank you, Mrs. Holmes," Sam said, feeling guilty. She hadn't even thought about her cat since she'd returned. She wished he was here—she could use a friend now.

"Oh, and if Mr. Spencer calls, I took a phone message for him this morning. A Mr. Delgado said his hotel reservation was confirmed."

Sam thanked her and hung up. Delgado! That meant Derek was going to Puerto Rico, and with Gloria! She didn't know why the destination should make her feel worse, but it did. She wondered if Derek and Gloria would stay in the bridal suite.

Making her mind a blank, she changed into the pink bikini and walked across the terrace and down to the beach. She swam out until she felt tired, then back. Then she repeated the procedure, longing to make herself so exhausted that she wouldn't care about anything but rest. She knew that if she began imagining Derek and Gloria in Puerto Rico, she couldn't bear it.

Finally she slumped down on the sand, watching

the surf. The ocean whispered its familiar lullaby, but for once it had no power to soothe her. She walked back to the house and made herself a peanut butter sandwich. She ate it standing at the sink, along with half a can of warm diet soda, tasting nothing. She stood in the shower for a long time, feeling the hot water begin to ease muscles stiff from driving.

When she felt she might be able to sleep, Sam toweled herself dry and reached into Derek's top dresser drawer for her comforting old football jersey. Instead she found the apricot silk shirt he had wrapped so tenderly about her shoulders. That seemed a lifetime ago.

She put the material to her face and the tears began. They rolled down her face as she buttoned the shirt, swallowed in its size. She started toward her old room, then stopped.

She was leaving here tomorrow, before Derek got back, but tonight she would sleep in his bed. Oh, Derek, I love you so much. . . .

Sam crawled between the sheets like a wounded animal, hardly daring to move. She felt as if her body ached inside and out, and yet the hurt wasn't physical. Pictures kept assailing her mind, pictures of Derek and Gloria on the beach in San Juan—and worse, in the bridal suite she and Derek had shared.

Shared? something inside her jeered. If you had *shared* that bridal suite, you might be together now.

But she couldn't have! Not then, not with the memory of Kyle. Now she was free of Kyle—and it was too late.

Sobs racked her body. At last, like a child who is cried out, she fell asleep.

* * *

A noise woke her. She glanced at the clock on the night table—one o'clock. Someone was moving around in the living room, she was sure of it. Derek? But this had a stealthy sound somehow.

While she hesitated, the bedroom door opened slowly. She strained to see, but all she could make out was a large form in the doorway, then moving into the room.

Derek would have turned on the light! she realized. She jumped from the bed and picked up the lamp, holding it over her head. "Whoever you are, stop right there," she said, shaking.

The light came on as Derek said, "Sam, I didn't mean to frighten—" He stopped, taking in the picture of her in his shirt, brandishing a bedside lamp against intruders. "It makes a better weapon if you pull the plug out," he said, grinning.

"Derek . . ." she said faintly, not moving. He wore a shirt of yellow silk and brown slacks. Her eyes drank in the sight of him thirstily.

He took the lamp from her hands and set it down. He touched her cap of black curls. "You don't look like Goldilocks to me. Aren't you afraid the big, bad bear will find you sleeping in his bed?" he asked, his voice low, his eyes searching hers.

"Oh, Derek, Derek!" she cried and flung her arms around his neck. He held her, surprised, murmuring soothingly as she sobbed against his chest. Her words came out with little coherence, "I don't care about Gloria, or Delgado, or anything but you. You're here, you're really here! And Kyle's gone, and it doesn't matter—nothing does, except I love you, oh, Derek, I don't care what happens as long as I can be with you, even Gloria—I love you, Derek!"

She babbled these things, the words muffled against his shirt, but the last part he heard clearly, and lifted her chin to look at her face. She saw a gentleness and love in his eyes that overwhelmed her, that she had only glimpsed traces of before. "Sam, my dearest love," he whispered, then his lips were on hers, pressing tenderly. Her mouth opened under his as he tasted her sweetness, his hand stroking her face and throat gently. Everything about him was so slow, so gentle, that Sam felt herself filled with love for him, this big, hearty man who could be so tender.

When he drew back she laid a hand on his cheek, feeling the stubble of his beard under her fingers. He smiled, toying with her shirt buttons. "I can see I'd better guard my wardrobe with you around. This is one of my favorite shirts."

"That's too bad," she said softly, teasing him. "You said I could have it—for my collection."

"Suppose I changed my mind. I might take it back, right now," he drawled, unfastening the top button.

"Like you changed your mind about our . . . business deal?" she asked, her eyes on his lips, watching them curl in a half-smile.

"A husband does have certain . . . rights," he said, unbuttoning the second button on her shirt.

"Oh, really?" she asked, with soft belligerence. "What rights exactly?"

His eyes met hers. "Whatever rights his wife wants him to have." He smiled. "What rights do you want to give me, Sam?" he asked, his voice husky.

She slipped the apricot shirt off her shoulders, letting it fall in a soft pool around her ankles, and reached her arms up to him. This time it was she who sought his lips. He stroked her breasts gently.

Sam touched her lips to the base of his throat, where the silver hair of his chest began. She slipped her hand inside his shirt, unbuttoning it. She looked up when he chuckled. "I am going to get *this* shirt back, aren't I?"

"Oh, you!" she said, pushing him away in mock anger. Then he laughed, that booming laugh she remembered from the first time she met him, and swept her into powerful arms, arms that were not so gentle anymore. Like Kyle? a tiny fear inside her asked. But this time Sam knew the answer: No. Not at all like Kyle. Like Derek—her wonderful Derek.

That realization seemed to break some long-standing barrier within her, releasing floods of feeling, floods that Derek's caresses turned into raging torrents, sweeping her to heights of passion she had never dreamed existed. His ardor no longer frightened her; rather, she gloried in it, reveling in her power to bring him the same joy she felt. She reached a miraculous crest of feeling, a dizzying height, and cried out. Derek's mouth smothered her cries, as together they rode out the storm.

Spent, she lay in his arms, intoxicated with the wonder of it all. When at last she roused herself to look at Derek, the smugness of his grin at first infuriated her, but then she decided his embrace was too warm and comfortable to leave in anger. She snuggled back into his arms, resting her head on his shoulder. "I thought you were in Puerto Rico," she said.

"Puerto Rico—how did you know about that?" he asked. A tiny, worried frown puckered her brow. So that was true.

She fought to keep the hurt out of her voice. "Mrs. Holmes said Señor Delgado called, to confirm your reservation. For the bridal suite, I suppose?" she added bitterly, then bit her lip.

Sam could hear a grin in his voice. "Oh, absolutely for the bridal suite."

"Hmph. What happened—couldn't Gloria make it?" The words seemed to jump from her mouth.

His chest began to shake under her head. He *can't* be laughing, she thought, propping herself on an elbow to look at him, but he was.

"You know, Sam, they tell me the best cure for a jealous wife is a cold shower. . . ." He stood and lifted her in his arms.

"Don't you dare—Derek, put me down!" she hollered, kicking her feet.

Now he laughed in earnest, standing her in the shower stall as he turned on the cold water, stepping in with her to keep her there. Then they were both laughing, and she was in his arms.

He turned off the water. "Ah, Sam, I've got to tell you. It's no fun, being jealous. I know—after Templeton," he said, scowling at her for a moment. "Gloria couldn't make it to Puerto Rico because I fired her."

"You fired her—but I thought—"

"The people in the office don't know yet, except Trudy. They think she's on vacation this week. Besides, Gloria also couldn't make it to Puerto Rico because she wasn't invited."

"Oh," Sam said, pushing a wet strand of hair from her face. "But Mrs. Holmes said you were going to the airport to pick up *tickets*, so . . ."

He laughed and kissed her lightly on the lips. "And did Mrs. Holmes also happen to hear where the flight left from?"

Sam shook her head.

"It was the five o'clock flight from Nashville, Sam."

"From Nashville—why, that's only—"

"It's the nearest airport to Hollyville, isn't it? What a coincidence! One might almost think the other ticket was for *you*, mightn't they? By the way, I like your father very much."

Sam looked up at him, her mouth open. "You went to Hollyville? Looking for me?"

His arms went around her in a wet embrace. "Yes, my darling, I did. And missed you by just a few hours." He took a towel from the rack and began drying her.

She stopped him. "Derek, about Jeff—there was nothing—"

"I know," he said. "I got back from Atlanta yesterday evening, and Trudy told me exactly what happened Friday. That's why I fired Gloria, and took the first flight I could get to Tennessee."

"Oh, Derek," she breathed. Then she shivered, wrapping the towel around her. "That *was* a cold shower, you awful man."

"Why don't we go back to bed?" he whispered. "I think I can keep you warm. You can even put on a nightgown, if you insist."

In the bedroom she reached for the apricot shirt. He chuckled. "Sam, aren't you ever going to wear that black, lacy number you got at Colette's?"

She reddened. "How did you know about that?"

"I saw it the night Fred and Agnes stayed here, remember? Besides, Colette told me she talked you into it. That's what she was whispering about as we left the shop."

Sam took the gown from the drawer and, with a shyness that seemed strange to her after what they had just shared, went into the bathroom to put it on, then returned to the bedroom.

Colette was right. That gown would never wear out.

ABOUT THE AUTHOR

ANGELA GADSDEN lives in Florida with her husband. They are both interested in Florida history and have a collection of military relics dating from the Seminole Wars. She is an inveterate doodler. When she takes pen in hand to outline a new novel, the margins of the tablets soon fill with sketches of the major characters.

Writing is immensely satisfying to Ms. Gadsden, an extension of the enjoyment she's always found in reading. "I can't imagine being without something to read for any length of time," she says. "The few times I've found myself in that situation called for an emergency trip to the library or bookstore."

In addition to books and writing, Ms. Gadsden loves cats, the ocean, college football, and soap operas.